Adrian Public Library

3 5201 60621 3976

P9-CSW-556

J Cutler
Cutler, Jane.
Susan Marcus bends the rules

JUL - - 2014

Premier
Selection

Susan Marcus

Bends the Rules

JANE CUTLER

Holiday House / New York

Text copyright © 2014 by Jane Cutler
All Rights Reserved
HOLIDAY HOUSE is registered in the U.S. Patent and Trademark Office.
Printed and Bound in December 2013 at Maple Vail, York, PA, USA.
www.holidayhouse.com
First Edition
1 3 5 7 9 10 8 6 4 2

Library of Congress Cataloging-in-Publication Data
Cutler, Jane.
Susan Marcus bends the rules / by Jane Cutler. — First edition.
pages cm
Summary: "As a New York-to-Missouri transplant in 1943,
ten-year-old Susan Marcus discovers a world of prejudice right
in her own backyard and makes a small but courageous
stand toward equality" — Provided by publisher.
ISBN 978-0-8234-3047-5 (hardcover : alk. paper)
[1. Friendship—Fiction. 2. Prejudices—Fiction. 3. Toleration—Fiction.
4. Family life—Missouri—Fiction. 5. African Americans—Fiction.
6. Moving, Household—Fiction.
7. Missouri—History—20th century—Fiction.]
I. Title.
PZ7.C985Su 2014
[Fic]—dc23
2013023665

For my grandson, Leo

CHAPTER 1

I was hanging as far as I could out of the third-floor window of my grandmother's Manhattan apartment and craning my neck to look west. I could see slices of the Hudson River through some trees, but across the river, the cliffs of New Jersey blocked my view of the rest of the country.

And I was yelling at Judy Wasserman who lives up on five through my empty soup can, connected by string to hers—homemade phones. I couldn't tell if they worked or not, because we were both yelling so loud we could hear each other just fine without any help.

"All I can see is New Jersey," I hollered.

"I told you," she hollered back.

Just then, my cousin Barbara tugged at the back of my skirt. "You're going to fall out and kill yourself," she said. "And don't yell out the window. It's not nice."

"I gotta go," I yelled, letting go of my phone so Judy could pull it up.

"Okay, bye," Judy yelled, letting go of her phone so I could pull it in.

The tin cans rattled down the front of the building and clattered onto the sidewalk. I ducked in fast in case anyone down below wondered who was throwing junk out of the window.

"Your dad is telling Grandma right now," Barbara whispered nervously, once I was inside. "They're in the kitchen."

I started for the bedroom door, and she grabbed my arm. "Nobody's in there but the two of them," she warned.

"Barbara," I said, "quit grabbing me."

Barbara let go. She's twelve, two years older than I am, but she's afraid of me. I don't know why. Anyway, she let go, and we tiptoed through the living room where two great-aunts and two great-uncles were dozing (we'd had our usual Sunday potluck lunch), and then through the dining room, where the bunched-up napkins were still scattered around on Grandma's big, claw-footed table. We got to the kitchen door just in time to see Grandma sink to the linoleum, murmuring, "Cowboys! Wild Indians!"

Daddy folded a dishtowel and tucked it under Grandma's head. Then he sat down cross-legged next to her on the floor.

"It's the dratted war, Mother," he explained. Grandma was my mother's mom, not his, but he always respectfully called her Mother.

Grandma opened a teary eye and gave him one of her looks. Daddy continued, "My boss, Mr. Pollock, has a bad heart, and he's been ready to retire for a long time. But he kept his dress-making factory open so his son, Dan, would have something to come back to after the war."

Grandma's eyes both were closed now, but she gave a tiny nod. "The thing is, Mother," Daddy said quietly, "Dan was killed in action a couple of weeks ago." He paused and cleared his throat. "So you see, now Mr. Pollock has no reason not to retire. Now he has a bad heart and a broken heart. He's closing his business. And I am out of a job."

My father had not been out of a job through the whole of

the Great Depression. He had not been out of a job since he quit school in the eighth grade and went to work to help his mom take care of his younger brother and sister. How could such a scary thing happen to him now, in 1943, when The Depression seemed so far away and the country was in the middle of a war?

"But I've been lucky," Daddy was saying. "I've found another good job. There's room for advancement, too, Mother. It's not just a job, it's an opportunity. Except it's in Missouri."

"In Missouri." Grandma groaned again.

"In Missouri," Daddy confirmed.

"Cowboys," she stubbornly repeated. "Wild Indians."

"Nothing of the sort," Daddy assured her.

"Poor Grandma," sniveled Barbara.

"Barbara," I turned to face her, "don't you know it's wrong to eavesdrop? You better scoot before Grandma finds out you've been listening to every word they've said!"

"Oh!" she squeaked, her hand covering her mouth and her eyes opening wide before she fled.

"Now, Mother," my exasperated father was saying, "remember what President Roosevelt said: 'The only thing we have to fear is fear itself . . .' "

Daddy admired our President and quoted him whenever he could. "I can't speak the way he does," Daddy had told me. "But the President and I think exactly alike."

CHAPTER
2

The next day, back home in the Bronx, I had to face a different problem with Missouri.

I was inside all morning, helping Mom sort through our stuff, when I got a message from Marv, my best friend, telling me to meet him later that afternoon.

Marv and I had different places around the neighborhood where we met. Secret places. Not that we needed them. We could just have met on the steps out in front of our apartment buildings and talked all we wanted. But we both liked secrets.

"In the alley," his message said, and when.

Of course, Marv and I didn't go into the real alleys, which were full of garbage cans and sometimes older kids. Our alley was a narrow passageway between two buildings with a fancy iron gate at the street end and at the other end, a big sink with a curly-headed baby that could spout water out of its mouth. Marv's little sister Rose would stand guard on the sidewalk outside the gate while he and I whispered together down by the fountain, which wasn't ever running.

We could always see Rose from where we were, dancing around and smiling. Anybody who walked by would know she wasn't just standing there for no reason. She was a dead give-away as a lookout. Still, she was part of the team. Lookout was her job. And she did it her way. That was one of the things I liked best about Marv. He didn't try to change anyone. If he gave you something to do, he let you figure out how to do it your own way. He might be able to do it better. He could do almost everything better. But he always let you do it your way if he wasn't going to do it himself.

That afternoon, my progress up the crowded avenue toward the meeting place was interrupted time after time. Friendly voices, some filled with emotion, telling me goodbye. These were people I'd known all my life—shopkeepers who had pinched my cheeks when I rode in my baby carriage. They truly hated to see me leave.

"And in the middle of a war," said Mrs. Alexander from the doorway of her bakery, "when so many are going." She sighed as she squished my face between her floury hands and kissed my forehead. "I wish you only good luck," she said.

I hugged her aproned middle and then rushed on, past the kosher butcher, the candy store with its bins of penny candy, the bagel store with fresh bagels on sticks, the fruit and vegetable market with its colorful wares displayed in crates piled on the sidewalk, the fishmongers, the deli, and the hole-in-the-wall Chinese restaurant where Mom and I and Marv and his mom and Rose would sometimes go for lunch, it was that cheap! I passed the tiny Hebrew School where Marv had begun studying for his bar mitzvah, which now I was going to miss.

Finally, I turned the corner and, down at the end of the block, there was Rose dancing with excitement at the entrance to the alley where Marv would be waiting. She opened the gate for me, then closed it with a clang.

Marv and I tucked ourselves away at the very back. "You're not going to have to worry about cowboys and Indians, Susan," Marv said, when I told him about my grandmother. "You're going to have to worry about Cardinals, and I don't mean birds!"

"I know," I said grimly. "I thought about that."

The St. Louis Cardinals had beaten our beloved Yankees in the last World Series, four games to one. And now I was moving into the heart of Cardinal country. Me, a diehard Yankee fan.

"The Cards and the Yanks both have great teams again this year," Marv said. "A lot of people are saying there's going to be a rematch for the series. What will you do, living out there?"

"Well, I can tell you right now, I won't be rooting for the Cardinals!" I declared. "I will always be a Yankees fan."

"Even when you're living in St. Louis?"

"Even when!"

"If there's another World Series between those two teams, you're going to be in a tough spot," Marv said.

"I will be," I agreed.

Marv looked down at his scuffed brown shoes and then at me. "It won't be the same here without you, Susan," he said.

"But no matter where I am, we'll still be best friends, won't we, Marv?" I asked.

Just then, Rose started dancing up and down like she had to go to the bathroom. "Hurry, hurry!" she called in an urgent voice. "I can see Daddy coming!" Their dad worked for the Post Office, and he got home early.

"Best friends forever," Marv whispered.

He stuck out his hand, and we shook on it.

"Forever," I whispered back.

Then we slipped out through the pretty gate, and Marv took the time to close it behind us.

According to plan, he and Rose went to the right, and I went to the left, even though we were all going to end up within half a block of one another when we got home.

CHAPTER

3

The huge train station was mobbed with servicemen in uniform. They were all over the place, hoisting their overstuffed duffel bags onto their shoulders and hurrying to their trains.

Our relatives stood in a brave band on the platform right near the train we were getting on—huge and black, with steam hissing out from underneath it.

Daddy took our suitcases to the compartment where we were going to sit and sleep for a couple of days and a night. He helped Mom and then me climb up the high stairs—there was a uniformed train porter, too, helping passengers to board. It was all a lot more confusing and scary than I'd expected, with our whole family assembled, waving, throwing kisses, and calling out their goodbyes—and my grandmother looking like she might fall over again.

Marv and Rose and their mom and dad were there, too, the four of them, standing apart, since they weren't family. Rose in front of her mom, smiling like always, and Marv in front of his dad, looking the way he almost always looked: serious, thoughtful.

Rose waved like crazy. But Marv just stared, like he wanted to fix me in his mind forever, just like I wanted to fix him. And at the last minute, right before the train gave its first lurch forward, while we were both looking hard at each other, he grinned and waved or saluted, or something halfway in between, a gesture all his own. And then the train lurched again—and Marv and everybody else were covered in steam, and we were off!

I was sick to my stomach the whole way—a thousand miles. And so was Mom. I hardly saw any of the parts of America the train passed through. In between throwing up, I mostly slept. And then we were there, in St. Louis, on the west side of the Mississippi River, where in early June, summer had already hit hard and the air was hot and wet and thick. And where people I heard talking spoke such a funny brand of English, I had a hard time understanding what some of them said.

Our new apartment was in a little town called Clayton, out west of St. Louis. It was on the top floor of a three-story building that didn't have an elevator. Not a single building in Clayton, Missouri, was taller than three floors, and only a couple of them—business buildings—had elevators. Daddy's new boss had rented the small apartment for us, not knowing that my mother would not be able to go up and down those three flights of stairs very often—not with her polio-weakened leg and her built-up shoe. In the middle of a war, places to live were as scarce as hens' teeth, Daddy said. We were lucky to have a place of our own and a roof over our heads. Period. I would just have to do a lot of extra running up and down.

That was fine with me.

There were two apartments on each floor. Only two! Skimpy. No long hallway like we had in our elevator building in the Bronx, with doors lined up and people you hardly ever saw living behind them. Just six families in the whole building! Across the hall from us, a middle-aged couple who had a son in the army. Below us, an older couple with a Scottie dog. Across from them, Mr. and Mrs. Jennings. She worked days at the airplane parts plant, and he worked there nights. Someone was always asleep at the Jennings'. And below them, an elderly couple who could not stand heat or cold. They spent summers in Wisconsin and winters in Florida and came back in between. My parents had never heard of such a thing. "And with a war on, too!" my mother said, shaking her head in disapproval. Then across the hall from this couple, three working girls who volunteered at the USO to dance with servicemen almost every night. I was the only kid in the building.

The street we lived on was right in the middle of a bunch of other streets just like it. Just lines and lines of little houses and duplexes and small apartment buildings, big front lawns and fenced-in backyards, driveways leading to garages in the back, but no shopping street. None. Not as far as the eye could see. And no real public transportation, either. No elevated train that turned into a subway, like we had in the Bronx. And the bus so far away, you couldn't even hear it. My dad hiked over to where it ran and took it to St. Louis, to work and back, until he connected with some men who had a carpool going and invited him to join. "Hardly anybody takes the bus," they told him.

That was not true. Every weekday morning, I saw women in white dresses carrying big black umbrellas opened up against the sun come slowly walking from the direction of the bus stops. Maids coming from wherever they lived to work at people's houses, to cook and clean and take care of children. I saw them again in the late afternoons and early evenings, walking back.

Here and there were big empty spaces, vacant lots, overgrown with weeds and brush. One large empty lot was right next to our apartment building, stretching from our house all the way to the corner. It was full of overgrown dried-out weeds and scratchy grasses. No place to play. But the men who lived on our block had cleared the closest end of it to make Victory Gardens.

Victory Gardens seemed to be the only thing anybody was doing to show that people here in the middle of the country knew there was a war on. That, and the girls dancing with servicemen at the USO. Otherwise, you'd never guess. Nobody had blackout curtains, like we all did in New York, and none of the kids wore identification disks around their necks—I got to take mine off as soon as we arrived. We didn't have buckets of sand on our roof to put out fires after a bombing, or air-raid wardens to warn us when one was coming. My dad was ready to volunteer to be a warden, but the men he talked to about it chuckled and said it wasn't necessary. Nobody is going to bomb Missouri, they told him. They will never get this far inland. They will bomb the coasts, and then they will get shot down. Relax, the men told him.

But the Victory Gardens were different. My dad got a small, leftover plot and a late start. But we figured if we dug right in, right into the reddish, clayey, unfriendly-looking soil, maybe we could grow some yellow corn by the end of the summer. We planted tomatoes and squash, too, which they told us would grow fast.

Just about right after we moved in, our next-door neighbor invited Mom over for coffee and confided to her that New Yorkers had a particularly hard time out here.

"Folks just do not like them," she told Mom, passing her a plate of sweets and filling up her cup. "It's because people from New York are loud and rude, and because they have such an ugly way of talking."

Mom was upset. She told Daddy and me later, while we were eating dinner. "I mean, she said it really nicely," Mom said, "like she had no idea how rude she was being!"

"I imagine she was just trying to tip you off," Daddy said. "To let you know in a friendly way what to expect."

Mom was silent. Her feelings were hurt. And on top of that, she was worried.

I was worried, too. I figured if I thought the people here talked funny, they must think I talked funny too. No so bad in the summertime. But once school started, watch out! I was going to have to get rid of my New York accent, and fast.

I listened hard, and I started imitating what I heard. Alone in my room, I practiced. In no time flat, Mom said that I was starting to sound like a hillbilly and to cut it out. So I knew I was on the right track.

Our block was full of boys, wild little boys with runny noses and summer haircuts so short they all looked bald. They were the kind of boys who ate Popsicles and let them drip right down off the wooden sticks onto their arms and hands. Boys who let gnats collect around the corners of their eyes. Boys who huddled around small radios in screened doorways, listening to baseball games.

I decided I was finished being friends with boys, and finished with baseball, too, so I spent my time helping Mom unpack, and drawing and reading.

Luckily, exactly a week after we moved in, Marlene appeared at our door. Her dark blond hair was just washed and still wet and pinned back off her face, and she was wearing a halter top and spanking clean white shorts that smelled sweet, like laundry picked right off the line.

When I answered the doorbell, she presented a plate of

home-baked cookies. "My mother sent these over to you all," she said, "to welcome you. She used up all her ration coupons for sugar and butter and baked this morning." And then Marlene smiled her glorious smile, and her sky blue eyes shone almost as brightly as the tiny gold cross she was wearing around her neck.

Mom came up behind me. "Ask your new friend to come in, Susan," she admonished. "Don't leave people standing out in the hallway."

"I wasn't," I objected, or started to, but Mom already had maneuvered herself around to stand between me and the sweet-smelling girl. "Thank you!" she exclaimed, taking the platter of cookies. "Please come in!"

Marlene stepped into our apartment, and I saw her glance around and take in the bareness of it.

"I have my own room," I said quickly.

My parents had elected to make the dining room into their bedroom. They put a drop-leaf table in the living room for occasions that called for a dining room. The three of us ate at a table in the kitchen.

"I got the real bedroom," I explained. Marlene followed me into my room. I saw her take in my twin beds. My tall blue chest of drawers. The makeshift shelves for my books and games and art supplies. The Yankee pennant decorating the wall over the shelves.

Her tiny cross winked. I had never had a friend who wore a cross. I could not stop myself from staring. She touched it.

"That's pretty," I said.

"Thanks," she said. "My grandmother gave it to me, and she likes me to wear it. All the time." Then she rolled her eyes. "You'll meet my grandmothers."

I did meet Marlene's grandmothers when I went to her house the very next day. They both lived with her, and her mother and her younger sister. They—the grandmothers—sat together at one end of the huge old dining table. One, her father's mother, sat in a rocking chair and read her Bible and mumbled. The other, her mother's mother, sat on a dining room chair with arms and a high back and knitted and read her Bible and muttered. And they both seemed to be put out about something.

Marlene's mother was in the kitchen cooking up a storm, her round, pretty face shining with perspiration. She had the same bright look Marlene had, and the same bright blue, friendly eyes.

Marlene's younger sister, Liz, looked like Marlene, but somehow, she wasn't pretty. She was a stocky, solid, freck-led, almost-seven-year-old kid whose dishwater blond hair was messy and needed washing and whose bare feet and legs could've used some soap and water, too. She hung around and pestered Marlene to play with her, even though Marlene had a guest. Then, to my relief, she disappeared. But not for long. The next thing I knew, Marlene's mom was calling, "Play nice with your sister, Marlene, honey. You girls play nice."

Marlene rolled her eyes. Liz stood too close to us—we were on Marlene's bed, looking through her huge collection of trad-ing cards—and said, "See?" Marlene stuck her tongue out at her sister, and Liz said, "I'll tell! I'm gonna tell!" and started for the door.

So we ended up all sitting on the floor, playing Chinese checkers, one of my favorite games, which I didn't have at home. It was better to play with three than with two, so I guess things worked out. But I understood that any time I went over to Marlene's, Liz was probably going to be part of the deal.

"The grandmothers favor her," Marlene told me as she walked me partway back to my house. "And if I don't give in to her, they nag my mother. She wouldn't make me do it if it weren't for them."

What about Marlene's father, I wanted to know. Did he favor Liz, too, when he was home?

"Oh, my father's never home," she said. "He's not here."

"Is he in the army?"

She shook her head, no. "Not really," she said. "Well, I guess you could say he is, sort of. Actually," she lowered her voice, "he's a spy."

"A spy!"

"Shhh!"

"A spy?" I whispered.

"I can't say another thing about it." She put her fingers to her lips. "Now hush."

"What does Marlene's dad do?" my father asked me when we were taking an after-dinner stroll around the neighborhood one evening. People had sprinklers waving back and forth on their lawns—and the spraying water had rainbow colors in it and looked pretty in the dusk. It seemed to cool off the still-hot humid air a little, too. Some of the water hit the sidewalks, and walking through the puddles felt good on my bare feet.

I glanced up at my dad. "Marlene says her father's a spy," I told him.

"Mmm," Daddy said, raising one dark eyebrow and inclining his head toward me. "What do you know about that?"

CHAPTER

4

When I was out of things I wanted to do or had to do, and Marlene was off playing with one of her other friends, I took the tennis ball Marv had given me as a going-away present—a Victory tennis ball with black seams instead of white ones—out back to the parking area, where the sheltered, empty garages stayed cool until the late afternoon, and played ball against the concrete floors and walls.

I got in a lot of satisfying throwing and catching, and I kept up a running story, like I was a baseball announcer talking about some outfielder going after balls he could almost not get. I called that outfielder—me—Crazylegs and threw the ball a little wildly, and made fun of me when I missed. And one day when I was doing this, and being super extra silly about it, I heard giggling.

Someone was watching me!

I went on playing, but I kept my ears open.

The giggling was coming from behind the raggedy hedge that grew beside the concrete driveway leading to the garages.

So after I snagged my Victory ball and stopped to get my breath and wipe the sweat off my forehead with the back of my arm, I ball-bounced my way over to the hedge and loudly remarked, "Hey!" which means "hello" out here. No answer.

"Want to play?" I asked. No answer. I bounced closer, pretending to concentrate on the ball but actually watching the hedge to see if any part of it was going to move.

It did.

Somebody who'd been squatting down behind the hedge stood up and looked over the top. A Negro kid in a tattered straw sun hat, wearing the same kind of denim overall shorts I was. "Okay," she said, disappearing for a moment as she stepped around the end of the weeds, down the slope, and onto the concrete of the drive.

I stared at her. She was the first Negro I had seen up close since we got to Clayton, except for Luther, the janitor, who lived down in our basement and clattered up and down the back stairs with the garbage cans a couple of times a week. He took care of some of the other apartment buildings on the block, too, but he lived in the basement of ours.

Luther was skinny and sullen. He always wore a long-sleeved shirt and a beat-up old felt hat pulled down over his eyes, no matter how hot the day. He wasn't friendly, but he was a good worker, which is what he was being paid to be, Daddy pointed out when Mom mentioned it.

"What kinda ball you got there?" the girl asked, holding out her hand.

"A Victory tennis ball," I said, not giving it to her.

"Can I see it?"

"If you give it right back."

"Okay."

I did not want to hand over my ball to a strange kid. But I did. She took it and examined it. Then she bounced it. "Bounce real good," she observed.

"Yeah, it does," I said, holding out my hand, "Give."

She bounced it again. And again. And then she started bouncing it all around and running with it.

"Hey, give!" I hollered, chasing her.

Her hat flew back, and I saw that her hair was braided into neat little rows all over her head. "Give!"

She was laughing to beat the band and bouncing my ball and running around the driveway on her skinny legs. And even though she was barefoot, she could run a lot faster than I could.

If I stopped chasing, she stopped running and just stood still, bouncing my ball.

"What did you say this here ball is called?" she asked me again.

"Victory," I said. "Give it."

"Victory," she mused, bouncing.

"Give it here!"

"What's your name?"

"I'll tell you after you give me back my ball."

"Mine's Loretta. But maybe I'll change it to Victory."

"Loretta, if you don't give me back my ball, I'm gonna—"

"What?" she mocked me. "You gonna what?"

"LO-retta!" came a woman's voice from behind the tangled hedge. "You give that girl her property back, hear?"

"Yes, Mama." Loretta bounced the ball to me with a friendly shrug.

I snagged it and stuck it in my pocket.

Loretta went and sat down on the weedy side of the vacant lot that sloped down to the cement. "So what's your name?" she said, patting the ground next to where she was sitting.

I hesitated and then went and sat down.

"Susan," I told her.

"You sure talks funny, Susan," she remarked.

"I do?"

"You don't sound like other folks. Not white nor colored, neither."

"I'm just learning," I admitted.

"Just learning to talk? A big girl like you?"

"I'm just learning to talk the way people here talk," I explained. "I just moved here."

"Where from?"

"New York."

"New York? Where that?"

"Where's that? You don't know where New York is?"

"Nope."

"You're kidding."

"Nope."

"Everybody knows where New York is. New York is the biggest city in the United States. New York is one of the biggest cities in the world. Come on, you do know, don't you?"

"Nope."

Loretta pulled a pale weed and started to chew on it. She waited for me to tell her.

I pulled my own weed.

"I have a map upstairs in my room," I said finally. "It'd be easier for me to show you where it is—on a map, I mean. It's hard to tell someone where something is. You know?"

Loretta nodded and chewed her weed.

"Can you come to my house? I live right upstairs in this building. I have a whole book of maps. Brand new."

Her face seemed to brighten.

"I'll ask Mama," she said.

We both got up and dusted off our seats, and I followed Loretta as she pushed her way through a briary little path that went right to the other side of the tangled hedge and led us to the most beautiful vegetable garden you can imagine: the early green corn already standing shoulder high to the woman who was hoeing the rich-looking soil around it; bean plants winding up slender poles; staked-out tomatoes that were still green, but big; melons lying on the ground, ready to grow and ripen; and tiny green-striped squash with yellow blossoms on the ends growing on thick, prickly, big-leafed vines. A secret garden!

A slender Negro woman wearing a loose cotton dress, men's worn-out shoes with the toes turning up, and an old felt hat stopped working and turned around when she heard us coming.

"Mama?" The woman looked hard at Loretta, and she did not look pleased. "Mama, this here's Susan."

"How do, Susan?" Loretta's mother said, looking at Loretta.

"Mama, can I go to Susan's to look at a book with her?"

"What kinda book?"

"A map book. She gonna show me New York, where she come from."

"Mmm," said Loretta's mother.

"Can I, Mama?"

Loretta's mother turned to me. "Your mama home, Susan?"

"Yes," I told her, "she's always home."

"And how she gonna feel 'bout you bringing this colored child to see your book?"

I was shocked by the question, but I kept my wits about me. I sucked in a deep breath, and then answered politely, "My mother will not think a thing of it. My mother is from New York!"

Loretta's mother appeared to be considering this, and while she thought, she glued her eyes to mine.

"So can I go, Mama?" Loretta nagged.

"Nope," her mother decided, turning back to her garden.

I was stunned. "No?" I said.

Loretta's mother slowly turned back around to give me a look that I cannot really describe very well—something between *Did you hear what I just said?* and *Are you still here?* With her eyes on me, she spoke to Loretta.

"Loretta, you still got work to do."

"Well, can you come over after you finish?" I asked Loretta.

"I don't think so," Loretta whispered.

"No, she can't," said her mother.

"Tomorrow?" I persisted.

"Girl," said Loretta's mother, "you know what 'no' means?"

"Well, yes," I said slowly.

"Don't seem like it to me."

"Are you saying no, never?" I asked, not feeling nearly as brave as I sounded.

"That's exactly what I'm saying," Loretta's mother replied.

Loretta had gone to kneel by the cut-flower bed over to the side of the small garden and was angrily pulling weeds.

"Oh. Well. Bye, then, Loretta."

"Bye," she muttered.

I started to leave, and then I turned. "I could bring the book down here to show you," I said. Nobody answered.

"Mama?" Loretta asked, furiously yanking at the weeds. No answer.

"Mama?"

"What?"

And that was that.

CHAPTER
5

The people who lived next door to us had just about everything my mother wanted. A big apartment with an air conditioner in the master bedroom and another one in the den. Thick wall-to-wall carpeting in every room. Fancy china dishes and sterling silver flatware. They had a mahogany dining room set and a console radio. And they had a baby grand piano in their living room.

"Gives us something to shoot for, babe," Daddy said, when Mom mentioned all these things to him. "By the time we're their age, we might have a lot of that stuff ourselves."

"Well," Mom said, "even if we had the money in the bank right this minute, we couldn't have it now, anyway. Nobody can buy luxuries like that with a war on."

Mom could almost always find ways to make herself feel better.

The piano was the only thing our neighbors had that interested me. The dark wood was so shiny you could see your reflection in it, and the black keys and the white ones were so clean and inviting, it took every ounce of willpower I had to keep from touching them every time I passed by, even though the picture of Allen, our neighbors' son, sitting on top, smiling, made me feel strange. Allen had been missing in action for more than a year. His parents hoped every day to get word that he'd been captured by the Germans and made a prisoner of war. But word didn't come. And nobody knew if Allen was dead or alive.

Mom told me to call our neighbors aunt and uncle. Up to now, *aunt* and *uncle* had been terms of affection, saved for people I was related to or people I really cared about who really cared about me. But here in the South, apparently it was different. Because I could tell from the way "Aunt Helen" looked at me and from the things I overheard her say about me to my mother that she did not care for me one bit.

"Look at those skinny little braids," she said to Mom practically the minute she laid eyes on me, giving one of them a sharp tug. And my mother turned all red—red! She was embarrassed. She wasn't annoyed with Aunt Helen for criticizing my hair, she was embarrassed about me. Oh, I was mad! But what did that matter? Mom dragged me to Aunt Helen's hairdresser anyway, who said, "Why honey, in this heat, you can hear them braids and ponytails hittin' the floor all over town—whamp, whamp." She said that—"whamp, whamp"— and I ended up with short hair and bangs.

And then, get this, Mom said to me, "I sure hope your hair doesn't grow out too quickly, Susan. That haircut was expensive." As if I had any control over how fast my hair was going to grow! And meanwhile, Mom saying that made me feel guilty, because I wanted it to grow out really fast and pulled on it every minute nobody was around. I didn't want to have to start a brand-new school with stupid-looking short hair and bangs.

But Aunt Helen was pleased as she could be and went around saying stuff like, "That haircut gives a little more body to her hair, and besides, she won't be chewing on the end of one of those braids anymore when she thinks people aren't watching, now, will she?" And then she looked at me and winked, like this is what the haircut was all about in the first place, to break me of some nasty habit. So the day I gave in to myself and touched the piano—one key, one measly white key—and listened with pleasure to the sound it made, so pure and beautiful—and then saw Aunt Helen scowling at me from the arched doorway to her living room, her feet in scuffs and her toenails painted a real mean red, I knew that we would never, ever be friends. I stepped away from the keyboard, and she marched over and closed the lid over the keys. Then I went home, across the hallway to our apartment, and she shut her front door behind me the same way she closed the piano: firmly. And we did not say bye, or see you tomorrow, or anything, even though we both knew that we would see each other again, probably even later that day, and all the time—all the time maybe forever, I thought unhappily.

And that's when I truly understood that *aunt* and *uncle* did not mean anything real in the South.

Every way I turned, it seemed, how to act or what to say tripped me up in Clayton. One night, my father and some men—neighbors—were playing gin rummy at our house and my mother and some women were playing bridge next door, and the front doors between the apartments were open, so people could go back and forth. The women were playing in Aunt Helen's den, in air-conditioned comfort. They were drinking lemonade with maraschino cherries on top and fresh ice cubes in each tall, frosty glass. I hung around for a while, listening to the loud hum of the air conditioner and the women's murmury voices and the clink of the ice in their glasses. I sucked on an ice cube and ate two of the sweet fuchsia-colored cherries. Even after Mom gave me the high sign, I lingered as long as I could in the long hallway that led through Aunt Helen's apartment to her front door, sliding slowly toward our hot apartment in my shortie pajamas, loving the feel of the soft carpeting under my bare feet.

When I crossed the tiled hallway between our apartments and came to say good night to Daddy, the first thing I felt was hot air and the first thing I heard was the sound of the electric fans the men had set up to blow on them in the living room and the radio tuned to the Cardinals baseball game. The men were drinking iced tea, and half-empty, sweaty pitchers of it were standing around. Some of them were smoking, and the air the fans were blowing about was not just hot but smoky, too.

As soon as I came in and walked over to the card table, one of the men took a smelly cigar out of his mouth, pointed to his sweaty cheek, and said, "How's about a good-night smack, little Yankee?" Then he winked at me and smiled, and when I stood frozen in my tracks, he pointed again at his cheek, right at the place where he wanted me to plant the kiss. "Right there. A Yankee fan and a Cardinal fan, making friends." He pointed to his cheek again. "A smackeroo."

Boy, was I tempted.

"No!" I cried. And I tore out of the living room and closed my bedroom door as hard as I dared to without getting accused of door slamming, which my parents did not allow.

I heard the men—not my father—laughing.

I didn't turn on my light, and I got down on my knees by the open window and looked through the branches of the big, old gray-barked tree growing right outside—so much tree, I could see only pieces of the tourquoise-colored evening sky.

"Oh, Marv," I whispered, "it's not just baseball that's the problem out here. It's everything."

I almost let myself cry—but I didn't. I just stayed there for a long time with my forehead pressed up against the good-smelling screen and thought about things.

The next day, my mother said, "Susan, you've got to learn to be more polite."

I considered this. "I am polite," I told her. "I am one of the politest children in the world."

"Excuse me," she said, "if that were true, we would not be having this conversation, now, would we?" I was silent. "Would we?"

"I don't know."

"You do know."

"No, I don't."

"Is that your idea of being polite?"

I was silent again.

"Now, Susan, when Mr. Bradley asked you for a kiss last night—"

"Mr. Bradley stank! He stank! He was sweaty and he was smoking a cigar! And I don't even know him!"

"I am not saying you should have kissed him!" Mom raised her voice. "Now, what did you say when Mr. Bradley asked you for a kiss?"

"He didn't ask me for a kiss. He asked me for a smack. And that's exactly what I should have given him."

"Don't be smart. What did you say?"

"I said no, of course. What was I supposed to say?"

"Well, you could have been more tactful."

"Tactful?"

"You should have said no in a nicer way. Girls have to learn how to do that."

"They do?"

"Yes, they do."

It was the first I'd heard of this.

"What do you mean, nicer way?"

I was sincerely curious. And I wondered, too, why I was supposed to be nice to a man who was trying to make a fool out of me, which wasn't very nice.

"Well, you could have said, 'I would give you a kiss good-night, Mr. Bradley, but I can't. I'm saving all my kisses for my daddy.' "

Mom was not joking. She was honestly suggesting that I should have said that silly thing to a rude, smelly stranger who was making fun of me right in my own living room. I could not believe my ears.

"You see?" Mom said, looking at me in an encouraging way. "Still no, but tactful."

I stared at her. "Why are you staring at me like that, Susan? Do you understand what I just told you or not?"

I shook my head, yes, even though I still wasn't quite sure I could believe my own ears.

CHAPTER 6

St. Louis is famous for a lot of things. For the great World's Fair of 1904, for example, where the first Olympics ever held in the United States were played. For having the two good baseball teams, the Cardinals and the Browns, and for the Cardinals beating the unbeatable Yankees in the World Series of 1942. For Eugene Field, the poet who wrote that poem about the gingham dog and the calico cat who fought until there was nothing left of either of them. He was born in St. Louis. And for the writer Mark Twain, who spent time in St. Louis.

But what St. Louis is most famous for, I think, is how hot it gets in the summer. Hot as—well, you know. I can't say it, or I will get in trouble, but the grown-ups say it all the time. Or the men do. The ladies say Hades, which means the same thing but is supposed to be polite. Kids can't even say that.

"What are we supposed to say?" I groused to Marlene. It was still morning and already so hot and humid that the two of us were sitting on my front steps without enough energy to do more than sweat.

Marlene giggled. "Grandmother Dennis says children can say, 'H-E-double-toothpicks'!"

"I don't get it."

"You know," she repeated, "it's hot as H-E-double-toothpicks!"

Oh, I got it, and I did not really think it was funny, but her good-natured appreciation of how silly it was was contagious, and we had ourselves a giggle and I perked up.

"The poor mailman," Marlene said, catching sight of him, "trudging all around twice a day every day in all this heat. My mother always gives him a big glass of lemonade with ice in it when he comes in the afternoon."

Marlene's mother, I had decided, was the cheerfulest and most considerate person in the world. Look at Marlene's toenails, for example, painted a shiny, beautiful pale pink. Her mother had just last night given her and crabby Liz a pedicure. Two coats of paint out of a brand-new Cutex bottle.

"Well, first she did the grandmothers' feet," Marlene explained. "They can't bend over enough to look after their own feet anymore, and their nails are all horny and hard to cut anyway. They won't let anybody do them but Mother. When Mother got finished with theirs, she said, 'Why don't you girls let me do yours, too?' She winked at me and whispered, 'It'll be real nice to do your sweet little toes after that.'

"She didn't mean anything against the grandmothers," Marlene hurried to add, "it's just easier to do ours. So we got our feet soaked in lavender water and rubbed with lotion and clipped and painted. Oooo, it felt good."

My toes curled themselves under so they would not show out the front of my sandals, but Marlene glanced at my feet anyway. "If you'd stop biting yours, I bet Mother would do them, too," she said. I was mortified. My toes curled tighter. "I never have known anybody before who bit their toenails, Susan," she continued, wiping the beads of perspiration off her high forehead with the hem of her playsuit skirt. "You might be one of the only people in the world flexible enough to do it. You're amazingly flexible, you know."

I was. I could do backbends and cartwheels and walkovers without thinking about it. I was practically made of rubber. I could put both feet up behind my neck if I wanted to. It was nothing to me to put my toes into my mouth and bite my toenails.

"You're about as flexible as a little baby is," Marlene continued. "It's a real gift."

"I guess," I said, "if you want to be in the circus or something."

"Or be a famous ice-skater," she said, "or a dancer."

"You have to be more than flexible for that," I reminded her. "You have to be coordinated. And have lessons. And be gorgeous."

"True," she said. "But you're very coordinated."

I shrugged. Maybe I was. But I had never tried ice-skating or dancing. And I was never going to have lessons. And it was perfectly clear to both of us, I would never be gorgeous.

"Anyway, it can't hurt to be flexible. When you're a grandmother," Marlene giggled and leaned on me, "you'll be able to polish your own toenails."

I giggled and leaned back. "Or maybe I will still be able to bite them!"

That tickled us both, and we had a real laugh.

The mailman brought a letter from my grandmother, so I took it upstairs, and Marlene came up with me. Mom was in the living room at the drop-leaf table, writing letters of her own. Two electric fans went back and forth, making their monotonous sound and pushing the warm air around. The window shades were pulled down against the heat outside, so it was dim and stuffy, but not yet unbearably hot in there.

"Red Kool-Aid in the fridge," she told us. "Help yourselves."

"It's really, really hot out today, Mom," I warned her.

"It's going to be a scorcher, my mother says," added Marlene, who lived on a first floor, which never heated up the way our third-floor apartment did.

"I know," Mom answered. "I heard it on the radio. Aunt Helen has invited me to come over later and sit with her in her air-conditioned den. She says there's no reason for me to stay here and roast when there is cool air only a few steps away. Isn't that nice of her? So if you need me, I'll be next door."

I nodded. Aunt Helen was so nice to Mom, and so not-nice to me. I was too hard for me to sort out the way that made me feel. I just tried not to think about it.

Marlene and I went to my room to see what we wanted to play with, and she spied my ball-bearing roller skates on the shelf. "Susan, I didn't know you had skates."

"They were in the last box we finally unpacked," I told her. "I forgot about them myself. They're pretty new, and I didn't even miss them."

"I love to skate!" Marlene said. "And the best place on the whole block to skate is in your garage where there's all that smooth cement. I'll go get my skates and we can skate down there."

"Are you sure it's okay?" I asked, thinking about Loretta and her mom, and the garden.

"It is," Marlene said, in a very positive voice. "Liz and I were skating there last spring and Luther chased us. And when I got home, Mother said Luther can't chase you away from there.

Only the owners of the building or somebody who lives there can chase you. And she said if he chased us again, we should tell him our mother said we could and if he didn't believe us, we should come and get her and she would tell him. But he never bothered us again. We skated over here a lot. It's a perfect skating rink. You'll see. Much better than the sidewalks. I'll go get my skates. Be right back."

"But wait—Luther lives in our basement. That's living in the building. He might have a right to complain."

"He doesn't."

"How come?"

"Because he shouldn't be living there. Everybody knows that. It's illegal."

"Illegal?"

"Against the law."

"I know what illegal means. But what's illegal about Luther living in our basement?"

"Negroes and white people are not allowed to live in the same buildings in Missouri. If somebody told, he would be in trouble."

This was news to me. "So why does the owner let him?" I asked.

Marlene shrugged. "I don't know. Probably something to do with the war, with the housing shortage. Let's not worry about it. I'm going to get my skates. Meet you in the garage."

I changed into hard shoes, the kind I could attach my skates to. But I didn't put on socks. Not on a day like this. I hung my skate key on its navy blue ribbon around my neck and picked up the skinny metal ball-bearing skates.

"We're going to skate down in the garages," I told my mom.

"Marlene says it's the best place to skate. And it'll be cool down there, too."

"All right," she said, not looking up from the letter she was so eagerly reading, or probably rereading.

"Mom?" I leaned against the archway that separated the living room and the dining room, now my parents' bedroom.

"Yes?"

"Did you know it's against the law for Luther to be living in the basement?"

She stopped reading and considered. "Well, I guess it is," she said. "I never thought about it. But segregated housing in Missouri is the law, so I guess so. Stupid law," she said. More and more, I could hear New York in my mother's speech. "Better get going. Pretty soon it's going to be hot as you know what, even down there."

"I think I'll take some Kool-Aid down in the thermos," I said. "Okay?"

"Sure," she said. Nobody from Missouri would have said sure that way.

I went into the kitchen and found the old red thermos we used to take to Far Rockaway Beach. Seeing it gave me a pang. And then I got the pitcher of Kool-Aid out of the fridge. The back door was open, and I heard Luther clattering up the stairs with the empty garbage cans. I remembered Marlene's mother and her kindness to the mailman.

"Luther," I called, "would you like some Kool-Aid?"

Luther froze. He stared in at me through the screen door. His felt hat had slipped back off his forehead, and I could see his whole surprised face. "No!" he cried.

As soon as he set down the cans and had a free hand, he

grabbed the hat by its brim and pulled it down to his eyes. Then he fled back down the narrow stairway.

But it was too late. I had already seen that Luther was not Luther. Luther was Loretta's mother dressed like a man!

My heart pounded and my hands shook as I poured Kool-Aid into the thermos and then wiped up what I spilled.

CHAPTER

7

Marlene was skating all around by the time I made it down there. "What took you so long?" she asked.

I sat down to put on my skates on the weedy slope I'd sat on with Loretta. I had changed into dungarees, to protect my knees in case I fell. But Marlene was such a confident skater, she was waltzing about in the same short playsuit she'd had on before.

She skated up to me and stood there while I fitted the skates onto my shoes and used the key to tighten the grips in front. One kept slipping. "Here," she said, taking her key from around her neck and handing it to me, "try mine." Hers did work better.

"Susan, your hands are shaking," she observed. "What happened?"

"Oh, I spilled some Kool-Aid and I had to wipe it up and start over, and I got upset because you know how sticky it is, and it was all over the kitchen floor, and I didn't want us to get ants and . . . anyway, I had to wipe it all up and wash the floor and then make some more, and I was in a hurry." I handed her the thermos. "We should put this in the shade so it stays cool."

Marlene took the thermos and skated majestically off into the darker part of the garage, where she stuck it behind one of the divider posts that went from the floor to the ceiling. I stood up, pushed off, and clumsily skated after her using my arm-swinging, city-sidewalk skating style, bent over at the waist and unsure of my balance until I had some momentum.

Marlene laughed. "You can relax here in the garage, Susan," she said. "Nobody here but us!"

"I know," I said. "I just have to get the feel of it again."

"Let's hold hands and skate together," she offered. "You'll get the feel of it quicker."

She took my hand and held it lightly, and then she showed me how to skate—nobody had ever really shown me before, I had just learned from trying and from watching other kids. But Marlene, in her good-humored way, showed me how to push and glide and pause. She taught me how to really skate. And suddenly, when I caught on, I was able to follow her easily.

We played tag and follow the leader. For the first time, skating was fun, not work, and it felt great. It was amazing, how much noise our skates made on that cement floor. At first I was worried about who might hear us, about who we might wake up or disturb. But then I quit worrying and just enjoyed myself.

Finally, overheated, laughing, and out of breath, we glided over to get a drink out of the thermos. And that's when we both saw her, standing back in the shadows, watching us.

Marlene looked confused and a little scared, and I tried to think of the quickest way to signal that it was all right. "Hey," I said.

"Hey," Loretta answered. "You two sure is good skaters!"

(I heard my mother's *sure*, which sounded something like *shoo-ur*, and now Loretta's, which sounded like *sho*—and then there was Marlene's, which I knew was *shir*.)

"This is my friend Marlene," I said. "This is Loretta, Marlene. She lives"—I caught myself and just gestured toward the back of the basement where the apartment was that belonged to the janitor—"here."

"Hey," Marlene said, picking up the thermos and pouring Kool-Aid into the cup. She took a drink and passed the cup to me, and I took a drink and started to pass it to Loretta.

"No thanks," Loretta said. "I ain't been skating my head off. I ain't thirsty."

Standing still, I realized that even the shady garage had gotten airless and stifling, it was that hot. We stood in the dark and looked out at the light, at the yellows and dusty greens of the vacant lot and at the burning hot cement—and saw that all of it, the whole outdoors, was shimmering in the heat.

"I'm so hot right now, I feel like I could faint," Marlene said. Her face was bright pink and shiny with sweat, and she gulped down another cup of Kool-Aid.

Loretta looked at her with concern.

"It don't never get real hot like this back in our place," Loretta said, "way back in the basement. It stays cool—well, kinda cool—even on a day like this. Whyn't you come in an' cool off?"

That sounded good to me. My whole skin was starting to feel prickly. I bent down to take off my skates, but Marlene just stood there.

"Inside your house?" she asked.

"Nobody home," Loretta said.

I could see a struggle going on inside Marlene. She just did not know what to do. I took my time with my skates.

Finally, slowly, she kneeled down and took off her skates, and the two of us followed Loretta through a door at the back of the garage and past big wooden storage lockers and the laundry room and the furnace room, where the little bit of coal that hadn't been burned last winter was still piled up against the wall next to the big black iron furnace, and then through another door that led into one large, dim room: bedroom, kitchen, sitting room, all in one, with a few tiny windows right up on the level with the sidewalk that were covered with newspapers and pieces of cardboard.

The room was nice and cool.

I had never been in such a shabby place before. Everything in that room was old and worn, broken and fixed, and rubbed shiny with use. But it was clean and neat and comfortable. Loretta had her own corner, with her own things, clothes and games and a few books on shelves made out of orange crates, and an ancient round rag rug on the floor under a child's rocking chair that she was too big for.

There was one double-sized bed in the room, so I guessed Loretta and her mom slept together. The bed was covered with a cotton quilt patterned in squares and rectangles made of all different kinds of faded material that looked like it once was people's clothing.

Loretta saw me looking at it. "That's called a crazy quilt," she said.

There was cold water in a milk bottle in the tiny, old-fashioned refrigerator, which was green and cream-colored and stood up on legs. Loretta poured a glass for each of us.

"It practically feels air-conditioned in here," Marlene remarked, going over to look at Loretta's shelves. "Oh, jacks! Who wants to play?"

We were all good jacks players, it turned out, and very competitive. Playing jacks on the cool cement floor occupied us for nearly an hour.

Then, quite suddenly, Marlene said, "I should go home."

"Okay," I said.

We all three stood up and walked back the way we'd come in, Marlene and I carrying our skates and the thermos.

Loretta waved from the shadows, and the next thing I knew, we were back in the bright, hot, late-afternoon outside world.

"I just suddenly had this feeling that Luther was about to show up," Marlene explained, as we walked around to the sidewalk in front of my house.

I was silent. I had no idea what to say. She went on, "Did you notice, there was only one bed? Where does Loretta sleep, do you suppose?"

I thought fast. "A rollaway, someplace," I said. "There must be one."

"Yeah," she decided. "You wouldn't think Luther would have such a nice place, would you? He doesn't seem to be the homemaking type, to me." Silence on my part. "Susan?" she prompted. I shrugged. "Well, I better be going. The grandmothers will want to know where I've been all this time!"

"What will you tell them?"

"Roller-skating with you, of course."

"See you tomorrow," I said, scarcely able to hide my relief as she headed off down the block.

"Bye-bye," she called back.

As I trudged upstairs carrying my skates, the thermos, and the afternoon mail, I thought about how unpleasant it was going to be in our third-floor apartment. No science teacher was ever going to have to tell me again that heat rises.

CHAPTER
8

A lot of times after dinner, in the lingering light, the grown-ups put out sprinklers on the lawns and we kids ran back and forth through the falling water. All up and down the block from lawn to lawn we ran, catching fireflies in glass jars as we went, playing tag and statues, hooting and hollering.

The women set up bridge chairs and a table, and the men their lawn chairs out of the way of the water and the kids. They brought out pitchers of iced tea and tall glasses, listened to the ballgame on the radio, talked, or didn't. The mosquitoes came and went, and the cicadas got louder and louder, and the greenish blue sky faded very slowly into black; and the sharp stars came out, and the pale moon.

"Those Cardinals," one man might say, "no stopping them now. They look stronger every game."

Then there'd be a pause.

"Surprising," another would finally answer, "with so many of their good players off in the army."

"Well, that's true for every team," someone else would chime in. "Every one of them's got to deal with that. The Yankees lost Joe DiMaggio and Phil Rizzuto, don't forget. And they're still playing great ball."

"Well, we've lost Johnny Beazley and Enos Slaughter,"

Uncle Lou put in, "and we're going to whip those Yankees again anyway. Just you wait."

The men chuckled. "Of course we will," they agreed.

My father was not particularly interested in baseball. But he was sociable. "Attendance at the games is up," he said, "since President Roosevelt requested more twilight double-headers to make it easier for working people to go. That was a good idea, don't you think?" Several of the men grunted their approval.

There was another long silence. "The war touches on everything," somebody said, in a way that was meant to wrap up the conversation. "Even batting averages. They're down, because baseballs are made with less rubber in them. Rubber shortage, because of the war."

Then there was a very long silence, and finally everybody gathered their stuff and drifted back into their hot houses where they fell asleep to the sound of oscillating fans or, a lucky few, to the hum of an air conditioner.

Sometimes I slept on the floor with a bowl of ice cubes near my head for a fan to blow across, and the cool air that made was as good as any air conditioner. I slept just fine.

The other thing Mom and Dad and I did was drive with Uncle Lou and Aunt Helen out to the airport, Lambert Field, way out in the country where nobody lived except farmers, so it was cooler out there already because of the darkness and the emptiness. Before we started, Uncle Lou would imitate the public service announcement on the radio, the one that encouraged people to be patriotic and not waste gas or tires: "Is this trip necessary?" he would ask in a radio voice. "You bet it is," he would answer, in his own voice. And we all would laugh.

Then, once we got to the airport, we would drive right out

to one end of the runway where a plane was about to take off, park, and wait. Soon the uptilted plane with passengers inside it would rev up, the men with the flags would wave it on, the plane would rev louder and spin its propellers, and then it would tear off down the runway at this terrific speed and when it came to the end, lift right up into the inky sky. It was thrilling to watch it. And besides that, it created a hot wind that blew right back at us, which for some reason cooled us off.

Another thing we did with Uncle Lou and Aunt Helen was drive way out into the country in a different direction, over a bunch of narrow, winding roads underneath big, old overhanging trees—my dad said you had to be a native to find your way there and back even by the light of day—to the watermelon stands. The watermelon stands were wooden picnic tables and benches set up in some clearing with a shack nearby and a couple of Negro men selling ice-cold watermelons, by the slice or the quarter or the half. The men were growing the melons in their own backyard gardens. You could never buy watermelon like that at a store. You had to know where to go, and how to get there, way out in the country.

Sometimes Daddy and I took a walk up to the air-conditioned drugstore soda fountain to get an ice cream soda. And almost every Sunday, the day he was off work, Daddy and I went to the swimming pool.

The Clayton public pool was huge and the most beautiful aquamarine color you could find in any watercolor paint box. The water was clear and clean. And it smelled delicious. Just the right amount of chlorine and sunshine mixed together. There were two lifeguards sitting in high white chairs right where the ropes and floats between the shallow and deep water were strung. Two older teenaged boys, suntanned, blond boys with bare suntanned feet and zinc oxide on their noses and whistles hanging on woven lanyards around their necks, or usually in their mouths—police whistles which they blew any time they saw the least little irregular thing going on in that pool, anything that got their attention, anything they thought could be at all unsafe. They were strict and watchful, and nobody, not even the silliest and wildest little boys, dared disregard the sound of the whistles, or they knew they'd be pulled out of the pool and maybe even sent home.

The Clayton pool had a big shallow end, an ample deep end, a low diving board, a medium dive, and a high dive. The wading pool was separate and surrounded by grass, so there weren't any babies or toddlers in the pool, not even in the shallow part of the shallow end.

My father was an open-water swimmer, so he had a strong, steady freestyle stroke, and nothing else. That was what he could teach me. But first I had to learn the basics. Daddy is a stickler. I had to prove to him I could put my head underwater and open my eyes. Then I had to float on my back and on my stomach. Since he and my Uncle Joe and I had played in the ocean together for years, it all went pretty quickly and before I knew it, I was dog-paddling around the shallow end, and then I could swim back and forth with him across the pool, somehow managing to keep kicking and coming up for air on my right side, the way he did, every other stroke. And then he took me right into the deep water. He said it would be just the same. And it was! Before I knew it, I could really swim.

Once I could do that, we invited my mother, who was scared of the water, to come to the pool with us and see me swim. Usually we took the bus to the pool, but this time, since my mother was coming, Uncle Lou loaned Daddy his car, and since we had a car, we didn't want to waste it, so Daddy let me invite Marlene to join us, and when Liz found out we were going to the swimming pool, she begged to go too, and Daddy said, well, after all, her dad is spying for all of us, the least we can do is to take her, and he had a gleam in his eye that showed what a good mood he was in, and so all of us piled into the car.

And then I remembered Loretta.

I had told my dad about Loretta before, and about her mom. And it turned out that he had already figured it all out on his own. "Let's keep this under our hats," he'd said. "It's hard for some folks to find work and places to live—especially in wartime, Susan."

And then he'd said, "Loretta's mother's name is Irene, in case it ever comes up. Irene."

And I wondered, how did he know that?

Anyway, I thought about Loretta when we were all piling into the car to go to the pool. I knew that Irene and Loretta went to church sometimes on Sunday mornings, and sometimes they didn't.

"Daddy," I whispered in his ear, "what about Loretta? Can I go ask her to come?" Daddy surprised me. He shook his head no. "No? Why not?" I said out loud.

"I'll explain later," he answered, and then he called out cheerfully, "Everybody in? Doors closed?" and off we went.

What a grand day we all had. My pale-skinned mom sat on a beach towel under a big hat, all wrapped up against the sun. She was in charge of the dry towels and the thermoses of ice-cold water and the zinc oxide. She established herself at the shallow end back by the chain-link fence next to the grass, which was as far from the water as she could get. But she smiled. "I can still see you," she said. "I can see everything." And she seemed happy to be there with us.

It turned out that Marlene was a graceful swimmer, and Liz could swim, too, as long as she kicked and churned and splashed liked an outboard motor on a boat. She had more energy than anybody, luckily, because she needed it to swim like that. But she managed.

After he watched us for a while to make sure we'd be safe, and made us play underwater tag in the shallow end until we got bored with it and begged to go into the deep water so we could play on the ropes and jump off the diving boards, Daddy let Marlene and me go. But he kept Liz in the shallow end. To my surprise, it was okay with her. She picked up some friends, the way you do in a swimming pool, and she was happy.

Marlene and I spent the whole rest of the afternoon jumping off diving boards. First the low board, then the medium one, and finally the high dive.

I had never done that before. At first, I wouldn't even consider the high dive. But Marlene said it was the best fun in the world and she said I would be so happy if I did. And was I a scaredy-cat? "Watch me," she said. I sat on the cement side of the pool with my legs dangling in the water, and watched all those kids swimming and paddling and horsing around, and listened to their happy voices, and saw my mother, so small now down at the other end, and my father, sitting with her, or swimming his steady laps, or fooling around with Liz, or standing nearer to the deep end with his hands on his hips, looking toward where we were, watching to make sure we were all right.

With the splashing and the happy cries and the chlorine and the sunshine and my eyes stinging and my back and shoulders starting to burn and my wet hair dripping water down my neck and the lifeguards' whistles blowing more often, more impatiently, the afternoon began to reach a kind of crescendo of activity and joy.

And there was Marlene waiting in line with the other kids to climb up the steep metal steps of the high dive. Going up step by step with big kids and little kids and finally getting her turn and walking out to the end of the board and standing suspended above the very deepest part of the pool and then with her arms spread out at her sides, just letting herself fall, pointed-feet first, and disappear! My heart lurched. The water was whitish down where she was. And the next kid on the board followed the rules and waited until he saw her come back up and sidestroke out of his path before he dived off the board— and she made her languid way right over to where I was sitting. She came smiling and breathless and shining in the sunlight— drops of water on her face and arms and shoulders, her blue eyes sparkling with pleasure and excitement. "Oh my, it was so fun!" she said. "Susan, you have to try it, you just have to!" And she was catching her breath and pulling herself out of the pool and standing over me and shaking her head so the cool drops of water fell out of her golden hair onto my hot skin, and laughing she grabbed my hand and pulled me up—and then we were running toward the high dive and the lifeguard blew two sharp short blasts and called, "No running!" and we stopped running and just walked fast, and then we both were standing in line and starting up the metal steps.

When Marlene was halfway up and I was just two steps behind her, I swung outside the ladder to see where my father was. I spotted him standing near the ropes that divided the shallow end from the deep, with a towel over his neck, one hand curled on his hip and the other hand raised to shield his eyes from the sun, watching us.

Finally, it was Marlene's turn. She started out to the edge of the board with a determined look on her face, and the way she stepped, one, two, three, and then bounced at the very end of the board, I could tell she was thinking about diving. Then she stopped, walked back, and started again. One step, another step, and another, bounce, bounce on the end of the springy board. Finally, she put out her arms exactly the way she did the last time and jumped into the water.

My turn.

I walked to the end of the board and looked down. The water looked really far away. I stood at the end of the board looking down for so long that the kids waiting got impatient. "Jump!" somebody called. "Dive!" "Jump!" "Get out of the way!"

I looked over to my father. He was still standing right there, with one hand shading his eyes, watching.

Looking down made me dizzy.

I made sure Marlene was out of the way, closed my eyes, held my nose, and with my heart pounding and my ears ringing with fear, I pushed myself off the high dive at the Clayton pool.

I hit the water harder than I thought I would. I didn't slip in smoothly, the way Marlene did, but sort of leaned forward a little so the water slapped my chest. And then I went down much deeper than I thought I would, too, deeper than I had breath for. I had been so busy being scared, I forgot to take a really big breath, and I was still somewhere near the bottom when I began to need air. I wasn't close enough to the bottom to push up off it, and I was surrounded by bubbles and stirred-up water, water stirred up by me, and it was not as light down where I was as it was up above me, and I began to claw and kick like crazy toward the surface, away from the bubble-filled paler water surrounding me and that I imagined was holding me down. I could not see anything through the churned-up water and the bubbles, but I could see the light at the top and just when I felt I could not hold my breath for one more second, my head popped through the surface and all the noise and the air came at me at the same time. I gulped the air and listened to the lifeguards' whistles and the kids screaming, and I realized that the forever it took me to swim from the bottom of the pool to the top was only seconds because I could see Marlene waiting for me, holding onto the side near the stairs, and she was smiling and not looking at all worried, and I knew that it really was only seconds since I dropped into the water and came back up again, and suddenly I felt exhilarated and strong and I smiled and paddled over to her.

"Wasn't that fun?" she asked.

"It was." I gasped. "Let's do it again!"

We hoisted ourselves out of the pool and walked as quickly as we dared—we could feel the steely eyes of the lifeguard on us—pulling at the bottoms of our soaking-wet suits as we went, shoulder to shoulder, across the hot cement deck, staying close to the edge to avoid the stretched-out towels of sunbathing teenagers. And then we were back in line at the high dive, where again most of the others waiting were squirmy, bony little boys, pushing at each other. Restless, excited boys who could hardly dog-paddle and just wanted to jump and jump and jump.

Before I knew it, it was Marlene's turn again.

Then mine.

This time, I strode out to the end of the board, took a huge breath, and before I could frighten myself, I jumped. I fell through the air and landed cleanly, going deep into the silence in a rush of white water and bubbles with my hair floating out away from my head and my eyes open in amazement. I had taken a big enough breath to last forever! Once I touched the bottom, I turned lazily onto my back and watched my own strong legs flutter as I gently kicked toward the light at the surface of the pool. I threw back my head so I could see my own arms reach up through the water, and as my hands and then my head broke through the surface, I let out my breath in one long, easy whoosh and swam over to the metal stairs, where Marlene hung, waiting.

"One more time?" she asked.

"Not today," I told her. "That's enough for me."

As I got out of the pool, I heard my father's come-home whistle. It was time to go.

We ran-walked back around the pool to Mom, Dad, and Liz. Liz was curled up with her head on my mother's lap, half-asleep, with her thumb in her mouth. As we came bustling up, Mom put her finger to her lips.

Marlene rolled her eyes and whispered, "Liz is not allowed to suck her thumb outside of the house!"

"I was never allowed to suck my thumb anyplace," I whispered back.

"You girls go get showered and dressed," Daddy said. We had left our clothes and dry towels in wire baskets in the women's shower room. The basket numbers we needed to retrieve them were pinned to our suits.

"What about Liz?" Marlene asked.

"Liz, too," he said.

Mom sweetly whispered little wake-up noises into Liz's ear, as if she were a toddler, and Liz started to smile around her thumb. Marlene rolled her eyes again. "Get up, Liz," she bossed. "We can't wait all day. Let's get to the showers before everybody else decides they want to leave, too."

Liz started to whine. "Marlene," my mother said, in a surprised voice, "you know that's no way to wake somebody up. It just makes them cranky. You can wait a minute more."

I just stood there, amazed, thinking about the impatient voice that woke me up most mornings.

"Come on, Lizzy Beth," Mom crooned, "wake yourself up, doll, and go with the big girls to get dressed, and then we'll get a hamburger and some french fries and a root beer float. Won't that be good?"

Mom knew that would get her. Liz loved food. She blinked and smiled at Mom and then she trailed after Marlene and me to the shower room, getting grumpier and more like her usual self every step of the way.

There was no explaining it. Mom doted on Liz, and Liz loved being around my mother. Daddy said it best: "They are an unlikely pair."

But he smiled when he said it, and I could tell that he liked Liz, too, and that it amused him almost as much as it annoyed me to see my mother and Liz playing cards at the kitchen table.

We walked through the warm, smelly foot disinfectant and then got our stuff from a cute teenaged boy who worked behind the counter, giving people their baskets back. He winked at Marlene and ignored me and Liz. "He winked at you, Marlene!"

"I know," she said. "It's his job. He's supposed to wink at one girl out of every three."

"Really?"

She nodded.

We all showered together and shampooed hard to get the chlorine out of our hair. Marlene said that she and Liz, being blonds, would have green hair if they didn't get it all out, but that since my hair was dark, it didn't matter so much. Mine would just be dry and brittle. I washed hard anyway. Dry and brittle on top of short with bangs—I washed. Then we came out and got dressed in the big open space with the long, wet wooden benches.

We were done in a jiffy, with our towels rolled neatly around our suits, feeling fresh and clean, tired and happy. Even Liz was happy—you could tell by looking at her and by how quiet she was and by how she did not drag behind us or ask a lot of annoying questions or whine about anything.

We did go out to a great hamburger place—we were hungry as bears from swimming all afternoon. And then we came home, sunburned and tired. And satisfied.

Later in the week, I remembered to ask my dad why he hadn't let me invite Loretta.

"Because swimming pools in Missouri are not integrated," Daddy said. "They would not have let her in."

CHAPTER 9

Going to air-conditioned movies was another way to cool off. In New York all the movies were open all the time, and you could go to a matinee any afternoon of the week. But in Clayton, we had one movie theater, and you could only go to the movies in the daytime on a Saturday or Sunday. Cooling off at the movies on a weekday wasn't an option.

Some kids went to the movies for the special kids' shows on Saturday afternoons. Only white kids went, actually. Movies, it turned out, just like swimming pools and places to live, were segregated. By law, no Negroes were allowed.

I didn't go on Saturdays. My parents liked me to go with them on Sundays. We went in the late afternoon and watched a double feature, and then we went out for dinner to a tiny Chinese restaurant my parents had found that was walking distance from the movie theater. It was a hole-in-the-wall-kind of place in an iffy neighborhood that reminded them of Chinese restaurants they'd gone to in New York.

The place had four tables and the man and woman who ran it didn't speak hardly a word of English. My parents thought maybe it hadn't been open for very long, because we were the only people who weren't Chinese we ever saw eating there. Sometimes we were the only people eating there, period. But we went every week after the movies, and the Chinese man, who was cooking, and his wife, who was serving, were always glad to see us. We couldn't read the menu or communicate in words, so we were never sure what we were going to be eating. But most of it, once it came, was good and reminded us of something Chinese we'd eaten before. We had black Chinese tea in little cups with no handles and beautiful blue-and-white plates that told a story of some sort—people crossing over a bridge, with willow trees and a fancy-looking house my mom said was called a pagoda. One time the wife tried to explain the story to me. All I could understand was that it was a story. And that was interesting, because I had never eaten off plates that told a story before.

Anyway, the movie theater was cool. AIR-COOLED, the sign on the marquee outside said in big letters. COME IN, COOL OFF. And there was a picture of a white polar bear standing on a big white ice floe surrounded by blue water. It did not really matter to us what the movies were. We just wanted to be inside, out of the heat.

But most of the movies were good. We saw *Bambi* one Sunday. And a funny one called *The Major and the Minor* about a woman who dresses up like a little girl so she can ride the train for half-fare. We saw one called *Yankee Doodle Dandy*, which was about show business. A double-feature—two movies— every time we went.

One Sunday, Mom and Dad invited Marlene's mom to go with them to the movies and the Chinese restaurant. It was okay with me. They were going to see something called *Casablanca* and some other war movie, and I didn't like the sound of either of them. I was going to stay over at Marlene's with Marlene and Liz—and of course the grandmothers.

Marlene's mom did not get to go out very often and she was thrilled. First, while she was still just in her slip, she put suntan-colored brown leg makeup on the tops of her feet and the bottom parts of her legs, and after it dried, she stood perfectly still in front of her bedroom mirror while Marlene and Liz and I sat on the floor behind her and Marlene drew black lines with an eyebrow pencil up the backs of her mom's legs, exactly in the center, so it would look like she was wearing regular nylons with seams up the back.

"Don't even breathe, Mom," Marlene warned. Her mother took in a deep breath and held it. I held my breath, too. And Liz got her face down so close to watch what Marlene was doing, Marlene had to elbow her away.

"Perfect!" Marlene said, when she finished.

Her mom let out her breath and looked back over her shoulder, lifting up one leg and then the other. "Oh, Marlene, honey," she said, "you did a great job! It looks like the real McCoy!"

"I could do it, you know," grumbled Liz.

"Next time, honey," her mother promised.

Then she put on a really nice dress, black with big white flowers on it, and red high-heeled sandals. She pinned a white artificial flower in her hair and put on bright lipstick, mascara, and then—scent! She put cologne on the insides on her wrists and behind her ears. And she put some on us, too. And while she was hurrying up and making sure there were tuna fish salads ready for all our suppers and iced tea and home-baked chocolate chip cookies and getting ready and being happy, the two grandmothers were sitting there at that big old dining table, in their usual places, begrudging her and not wanting her to go. Just about a minute before my father was supposed to come to pick her up, Grandmother O'Brien said, "Mary," and Marlene's mother said, "Yes, Mother O'Brien?"

And then the grandmother said in a furious whisper, "I don't see how you can do this, Mary."

And Marlene's mother stopped getting ready and said, very pleasantly, "Do what, Mother O'Brien?"

And then the grandmother just practically spit it out, "Go out with those people! You know that man is a Jew!"

And then Marlene's mother froze and put her hand over her heart. I don't think I have ever seen anyone look quite so upset since we told my grandmother we were moving away. "Mother O'Brien, what a thing to say," she said, "and right in front of the children!"

I felt bad, seeing her so upset. I felt like I just had to try to help her out. "It's all right," I said. "Don't worry. I am one, too, you know. And so is my mom."

Then Marlene's mother turned and looked at me, and how mixed-up she was feeling was written all over her face. I could tell she was almost ready to cry—and just then, the doorbell rang, and it was my father.

She pulled her face together, fluffed her hair, and hurried down the hallway to let him in.

Daddy strode into the living room, winked at us kids, and then went right over to the grandmothers. "How do you do, Mrs. Dennis, Mrs. O'Brien," he said, standing before them, not too close and not too far, and bowing over them a little, as if he were greeting queens. "I hope these three girls take good care of you tonight."

Both grandmothers looked confused. Grandmother Dennis squinted up at him. "You young people enjoy your evening," she croaked. "My Mary doesn't get out near often enough. Don't you worry about us. We'll be fine."

Grandmother O'Brien glowered and did not answer him.

"We'll be off, then," Daddy said. He kissed me on top of my head and waved to Liz and Marlene. "Are you sleeping over here," he asked me, "or do you want to come home with me when I bring Mrs. O'Brien home?" I had been planning to sleep over, something my mother almost never allowed me to do, but I changed my mind.

"I'll go home with you," I told him.

"Could be late," he warned.

"That's okay. If I'm asleep, you can carry me."

He pretended to be alarmed. It was a joke between us now, about how he could barely pick me up anymore, and when he did, he could not keep my feet from dragging along the ground.

So off they went.

Marlene and Liz and I retreated to their bedroom to look through a new book Marlene's mom had gotten for them called *Being Born*, which supposedly told all about where babies come from. Before we could get to it, Grandmother Dennis was hollering for Marlene to come and get dinner on the table.

I was not in the mood to have dinner with the grandmothers. But I had no choice. As it turned out, nobody said a single word all through dinner. It was the silentest meal I ever ate. Nobody even asked anybody to pass the homemade buttermilk biscuits. Marlene just passed them and then she passed the honey and poured the iced tea and the instant we were all finished eating, she jumped up and cleared the table and said that Liz and I were excused, and we left and went back to *Being Born*.

And that was that.

The grandmothers took themselves to bed early, like they always did.

We were less interested in *Being Born* than we thought we would be. The book talked a lot about animal babies and hardly at all about all the things we wanted to know about, so we played a long game of Monopoly instead. While we were playing, Marlene said, "Oh, by the way, Liz told me about Luther."

I kept my eyes glued to the board. "What about Luther?" I asked.

"I mean, about Loretta's mom," she said, "you know."

"I do?"

"Of course you do," Liz said, impatiently. "Everybody does."

I looked at Marlene, into her blue, clear eyes. "Do they?"

"They do," she said, "since Liz found out and told them."

"How did you find out, Liz?" I asked.

Liz shrugged and did not answer. Marlene rolled the dice. "Liz is a natural-born snoop," she reminded me.

After Marlene and Liz went to bed, I fell asleep in my clothes on the loveseat in the living room, which is where Daddy found me when he brought Mrs. O'Brien home.

As he and I strolled home, I got wider and wider awake. It was extremely pleasant, walking right down the middle of the familiar street, unfamiliar so late at night under the different-looking stars and the differently placed moon.

"Did you have a nice time?" I asked.

"We did," he said. "Very nice. Good movies. And

Mary—Mrs. O'Brien—had never eaten Chinese food before. So that was fun. You?"

"It was okay. Except for the part about Grandmother O'Brien being mean about you being a Jew. Did you hear about that?"

He had not, so I told him.

"Some people are like that," he said. "It can be a problem."

I leaned against my father as we walked.

"How many nylon stockings do you think it takes to make a parachute?" I asked him.

"No idea," he said. "A lot."

"Are you going to get drafted and have to fight in the war?" I asked him.

"Looks like I won't," he said. "I probably would have been, if we were still in the Bronx. Uncle Joe wrote me that the draft board there has started taking men with children. But here in Clayton, the draft board is loaded with young, single men. It's nowhere close to drafting married men, let alone men with children. And I'm almost too old to be drafted anyway."

How comforted I felt. Whatever else I thought about moving to Clayton, this was one very good thing. My father was not going to get drafted and leave us and be in danger and maybe turn up missing in action, like poor Allen, who smiled and smiled at everybody from the top of the piano, but who was always still missing.

CHAPTER
10

Rolling thunder and heat lightning in the night, and then a steady rain, which rushed along the roof over our heads all day long—it was a welcome break from the heat.

Fresh, sweet smells poured in through our screened, open windows. Mom and I were content indoors. She did chores, listening to her soap operas on the radio, and then she sat down at the dining table in the living room and scribbled away, only stopping to refill her fountain pen with ink. Now Mom was not only writing to friends and relatives back east, but also to servicemen overseas. It was a project she worked on for the Red Cross. Every man in uniform needed to get as much cheerful mail from home as he could, and some of them had no relatives or even friends to write to them. I don't know how many soldiers my mother had taken on, but the project kept her busy and gave her pleasure. And she was fulfilling her patriotic duty, too.

I read a Nancy Drew mystery, one of the five books—the limit—I'd gotten at the library on Saturday. I sat on the floor right underneath one of the windows in my bedroom. Every once in a while, a cool raindrop splatted through a hole in the screen and onto the back of my neck.

"I'm writing to Aunt Lil today, Susie," Mom called. "Do you want to put in a note to Marv and Rose?"

"Sure," I called back.

I quickly closed the book and got a pencil and some blue-lined notebook paper I'd saved from school last year. I sucked on the eraser end of my pencil. I had way too much to say to Marv to write in a letter. Even if I could talk to him on the telephone, which I could not, since it would cost an arm and a leg, as my dad would say, I wouldn't be able to tell him everything I wanted to. For that, I'd have to see him in person. And I knew that was probably never going to happen again. I shook my head to get rid of the thought.

Dear Marv, I wrote,

You were right about baseball. I am the only Yankee fan in town. So I just do not bother with baseball. I have other stuff to worry about. One thing is trying to get rid of my New York accent before school starts. Another thing is Jim Crow. That is the name they give to laws they have to keep Negroes and white people separated from each other. Can you believe it? I would love to do something against old Jim Crow, but I don't know what. What could a kid do against laws like that, anyway? And one more thing. I have an ugly haircut that I hope will grow out in time for school.

Please write back!

Still Your Best Friend,
Susan

Then on the back of the paper, I wrote to Rose:

Dear Rose,
Guess what? They have all the same radio programs here. I listen to Let's Pretend *every Saturday morning. Think about me when you listen. It will be like listening together.*

Your Friend,
Susan

I folded the paper over and over for privacy, and gave it to Mom, and hers and mine all went to New York in the same envelope, with the same three-cent stamp.

I got my answers back in no time flat. MISS SUSAN MARCUS, the envelope said, written in Marv's elaborate cursive, and inside, two separate pieces of paper, one folded crookedly, one perfectly.

Rose sent me a crayon picture of a smiling girl wearing a blue triangle for a dress with black stick legs and black stick arms and five stick fingers on each round hand. The girl's arms were stretched out, ready to hug, and on her round face were black dots for eyes and a big U-shaped smile. At the bottom of the page, Rose wrote xoxo and then her name in wandering blue letters.

Marv had drawn a picture of an evil superhero named Jim Crow, part bird, part man: a monster, facing front and looking straight out. He had a tiny bird's head with a big, sharp yellow beak; hunched wide red-winged shoulders and red feathers down to the elbows and enormous muscular black leather arms and leather-gloved hands below that. His huge chest was covered with black leather, too, and so were his big thighs. But the lower part of his legs, though they were spread wide in a menacing stance, were small and covered in feathers. Behind him hung a long cape made of more red feathers. You could see that Jim Crow was ready to fight. He was ready to jump right off the page and attack you.

Down at the bottom of Marv's picture were children, white kids and colored ones, all looking scared. And up near the top, near the Jim Crow superhero's shoulder, kind of hanging out in space, was me, with my dark hair in braids the way it used to be. I was holding a peashooter up to my mouth, and a homemade slingshot hung out of my back pocket. Above my head were fancy words enclosed in a zigzag box that said, TAKE THAT, JIM CROW! And then at the bottom of the picture in bold letters, it said, SUSAN MARCUS MEETS JIM CROW.

Marv was a wonderful artist.

After I finished just enjoying the picture, I studied it, to see what made it so good. Jim Crow, all black and red, had the meanest little bird eyes and the meanest old bird beak you can imagine. And there was something about that tiny head up on top of that big hunk of a body that made him extra scary—because it made you know he was all muscle and meanness and no brain. I studied the drawing for a while more. Then I folded it back up and put it away in my cigar box and then in my middle drawer, underneath my pajamas. I wanted to keep it to myself.

"What did the kids have to say?" Mom wanted to know. I showed her Rose's picture. "Cute," she said. "And what about Marv?"

"Private," I told her.

CHAPTER
11

One odd thing about the way Jim Crow worked in St. Louis: the buses weren't divided. In other segregated cities, Daddy told me, Negroes had to sit in the back part of the bus. But in St. Louis, anybody could sit anyplace they wanted on buses and streetcars. "Probably because Missouri is a border state," he said.

"What's that?" I asked.

"During the Civil War, it was one of the slave states that bordered the North. The population was pretty much divided in their support between the North and the South. Even now, that division of opinion will show up in funny ways. Like a lot of Jim Crow, but not all Jim Crow." For a Canadian, my dad knew a lot about American history.

"The laws here are a lot different than they are in New York, eh?"

"And the way people talk is, too," I added.

Public transportation—buses—not being segregated interested me. But when I began my scheming about how Marlene and Loretta and I could pull a fast one on Jim Crow, the first thing I thought about was the swimming pool. Just run right over old

Jim Crow, I thought. What would anybody dare do to three sweet little girls who innocently broke the rules?

We were playing Monopoly down at Loretta's one broiling afternoon, and I waited until Loretta got Park Place and Marlene put a hotel on Marvin Gardens, so they both would be in a good mood, and then I got up and got some more sun tea out of the fridge—Irene made tea by leaving the pitcher of water with the tea bags outside in the sun in her Victory Garden—and when I sat back down I said in my most offhand way, "I bet we could get you into the Clayton pool, Loretta." Then I took a long swallow and pretended to be studying the board.

Loretta and Marlene both stared at me like I was from another planet.

"Come again?" Loretta said, finally.

"I said—"

"We heard what you said!" Marlene interrupted. "What in the world can you be thinking, Miss Susan New York Marcus?"

"I am thinking that if we just went over to the pool and paid our money and walked in like we didn't know any better and . . . well, what would they do, those boys who work at the pool? Call the police to come put three innocent little girls in jail or something?"

"Yes!" Marlene exclaimed. "They would! They would have to! It is the law, Susan. Are you out of your mind?"

Loretta was still just staring at us. "Do you think they would, Loretta?" I said.

"I think you been outside in the heat too long this morning, girl," Loretta said. "First off, they wouldn't let me in that pool, not in a million years. Second, if they did, what you think my mama would do to me, I came back here smelling the way the two of you smell after you been sloshing around in the chlorine? And third, what make you think I would even want to stay out in the hot sun all day with nothing on? Ain't I black enough to start with? And fourth, naw, I don't think they would put three innocent little girls in jail. I think they would put one innocent little girl in jail. One innocent little colored girl. Me. The answer is no! The law say no. And I say no." Loretta looked angrily at me. "Now take your turn," she said.

Loretta had said no in so many ways and for so many reasons I could hardly sort it all out. But while I was trying to, Marlene added, "Nobody's going swimming any more this summer anyway. Tomorrow's August first."

August first! I had been so occupied with scheming, it had slipped my mind—the all-important date. The day the swimming pools would shut down because of polio. Nobody was sure how polio spread, but it might be through the water at crowded pools. And August was the month a lot of people came down sick with it. Swimming was over for everybody.

"August first!" I exclaimed. "We should have gone swimming today!"

Marlene sighed, rolled the dice, and moved the shoe, which was my piece, five spaces ahead.

"Don't make no sense to me," Loretta complained, "closing the swimming pools. Colored kids get polio, and they don't have no pools to go to."

"It's crowds," Marlene said. "You know, kids can't go to the movies, either."

Loretta shrugged. "Colored kids can't go to movies, Marlene, and they still get sick. You see what I'm sayin'?"

Marlene bit her lower lip and passed the dice to Loretta. "Your turn," she said.

No swimming and no movies in August, and everyone said

it was by far the hottest part of the summer. Loretta took her turn, Marlene took hers, and I took mine.

"Where do you tell your mama you're at when you're playing over here, Marlene?" Loretta asked.

"I tell her I'm at Susan's," Marlene said.

"And she always believe you?"

"Of course she does." Marlene looked indignant. "Everybody at my house knows that I am completely truthful!"

I had lost interest in the game. "I quit," I said. "Let's think of something else to do." I stretched out on my back and looked up at the network of pipes that crisscrossed the low ceiling of Loretta's basement home.

"I don't know why you take it all so personally," Marlene said. "Loretta is the one who should take it personally, and she doesn't."

"Is that true?" I asked Loretta. "Don't you?"

She was putting away her Monopoly game and she didn't answer right away. "I do and I don't."

We waited.

"But since there ain't nothin' I can do about it, I just try not to think about it. I mean, it really is not that simple, Susan. First off, there's the law. And second, I am not so sure I want to be running all over the place where white folks is. I mean, even if they wouldn't hurt me, it would just feel funny. You know?"

I sat up. "It doesn't feel funny for you to be with us!" I protested.

"It might, if we wasn't here in my own house."

"It might," agreed Marlene.

"For you or for her?" I asked.

"Well, for me, I meant," she admitted.

66

"See?" said Loretta, pointing her finger at Marlene.

"She did not mean that, Loretta," I said.

"Of course I did," Marlene said.

"She did, too," Loretta said.

They both turned on me. "Okay," I said. "I just thought you didn't."

"We do not say things we don't mean," Marlene said.

"No, we don't," Loretta agreed.

"Excuse me," I said sarcastically.

Everyone was silent.

"So where were we?" I asked.

"We were nowhere," said Marlene.

"And we ain't going nowhere, neither," said Loretta.

"Right," said Marlene. "And if you want to take on Mr. Jim Crow, you can just leave us out of it. Right, Loretta?"

"Amen," said Loretta.

They both stretched out on the floor. Arguing seemed to make everybody want to lie down.

"Your daddy really a spy?" Loretta asked Marlene after a while.

"Maybe," Marlene said. "I don't know. He's something."

"Everybody something," said Loretta. "But is he a spy?"

"I don't think so," Marlene admitted, "but when he left, we had to tell Liz something, and that's what Mom told her. We couldn't just say he left us."

"How come?"

"It would have hurt her too much."

"Luther left us," said Loretta.

"Why?" I asked.

"Mama say maybe he joined up to fight," Loretta said. "But we don't know for sure."

Marlene giggled and turned over on her side so she could look at Loretta. "I bet he's a spy, too, Loretta."

Loretta smiled. "Could be," she said. "How come your daddy not a spy?" she said to me.

"He is a spy, Loretta," I told her, keeping my eyes on the ceiling. "What'd you think?"

One day, Irene told Loretta that the three of us could pick the ripening tomatoes and some of the small ripe corn and zucchinis out of her garden and take them home. "We got too much for just us and we got plenty to take over to the church, too. Most ever'body there got gardens of they own, anyway," she added.

I had seen Irene looking over at the puny Victory Gardens my father and the other men had scratched out. Not one of them was flourishing. And Daddy's, with his late start, was the saddest one of all.

"Mmm, mmm." She shook her head with pity and then came back to tell us to come and take some of her crop home.

So there we were in the garden under a searing sky, harvesting. I held a warm pinkish tomato in my palm and smelled it before I set it in my basket. I stood between the rows of corn and listened to how the drying leaves protested, rustling when I pulled at the stalks and looked to see if any ears of corn were mature enough to pick, the way Loretta showed me.

Harvesting vegetables in the heat was peaceful and pleasant. The three of us worked quietly, until Loretta said, "There must be something we can do for fun except just hide out in the basement till I leave."

"Leave?" I asked her, in a sun-soaked, dreamy voice. "What are you talking about?"

"I mean something better. Maybe something to get back at old Jim Crow. Without getting ourselves in trouble," she quickly added.

"But where are you going?" Marlene came out from between two rows of cornstalks and stood over Loretta, who was squatting to look for ripe zucchinis beneath their broad, protective leaves.

"To Arkansas, to live with Gran."

"But what about school?" I objected.

"You think they ain't schools in Arkansas?"

"Well, no, I mean—" I wasn't sure what I meant.

"I'll go to the same kinda school as here, one room, one teacher, kids from kindygarten through grade eight, old worn-out books. It'll be exactly the same."

"But you won't know anybody!"

"Course I will. I got a million cousins live right there by Gran, and aunties and uncles. I been down there lots of times."

"What about Irene?" Marlene asked.

"Mama's going to California," said Loretta, frowning. "She gonna get herself a job in one of them war plants they got out there in Oakland. Lots of women working building ships, doing jobs men did before the war, and making real good money. Mama going out there. And then after she get herself settled, maybe I can go live with her. Or maybe I just stay with my folks in Arkansas."

"It's hard to move," I said.

"Not if you move to someplace you've been before and where you have a grandmother and a million cousins," practical Marlene observed.

"Is that really what your school is like here?" I asked.

Both of them nodded, yes.

I turned back to my harvesting, shocked and embarrassed. Mom and I had gone to my new school, the neighborhood school, the white school, just a few days before to meet the principal and get me registered. It was a long two-story building with a sloping, perfect green lawn in front and a giant playground off to one side. The classrooms were big and airy with blackboards covering two walls, huge windows covering another, and bulletin boards and bookcases on the other. And each classroom had its own small art room with a sink and cupboards that went all the way up to the ceiling, full of supplies. Each classroom had its own cloakroom, too, with hooks for coats and cubbies for lunches and a bat-and-ball box. And then there was the teacher's big desk and chair, and all the students' desks with chairs attached to them and hinged desktops that opened and closed and had a groove for pencils and pens and a hole for the inkwell. And the principal showed Mom and me the textbooks we'd be using in the fifth grade this year—and the readers and the math books were brand-spanking new.

And when we left, Mom said, "Would you believe that was the principal himself who showed us all around? Would you believe how wide and light those hallways are? How fresh the paint is? How big the bathrooms are? Would you believe how few students there will be in each of those classrooms? Oh, Susan, that is the best school I ever saw in all my life! And that nice man—that actually was the principal, and he hugged you and called you by name!"

Mom was kind of breathless, telling Daddy about the school that night.

"What did you think about the place, Susie-Q?" he asked me.

"I liked it," I told him.

Of course, I liked my old school better. Even though it did

look like a brick prison and had almost no room in the yard to play and certainly no grass. I knew the kids there, and I had friends. And I was president of my fifth-grade class—or would have been president, if I had stayed.

"I'll probably like it more when kids are there," I allowed.

Daddy smiled. "I imagine you will," he agreed.

But when I heard about Loretta's school and remembered how grumpy I'd been about mine, I felt embarrassed and I hid my unappreciative self in the rows of corn until I could be sure the mixed-up emotions I was feeling weren't written all over my face. Then I doubled back to what she'd said.

"I can think of one thing we could do that would sort of get at Jim Crow that wouldn't get us into trouble," I said. "I'll tell you later."

When we'd finished, we sat at Loretta's kitchen table, drinking sun tea and eating mayonnaise-and-white-bread sandwiches with fresh slices of the one really ripe tomato we'd found, still warm from the garden. Irene was working over on a different block, and there was no chance she would be home soon. Even so, we leaned together and spoke softly, as if the walls might have ears. "First off," I said, "buses and streetcars are not Jim Crowed in St. Louis. Or in Missouri, either."

"But it seems like they are," Marlene said. "I mean, Negroes and white people never sit together."

"But they could. We could. And we wouldn't be breaking any law. We would just be doing things differently from how they're done."

"Are you sure?" Loretta asked.

"I am. I talked to my father."

"About what?" they asked together, both sounding alarmed.

"Not about us! About the law. About whether white

people and colored people are allowed to ride together on the buses here. Whether there is Jim Crow on public transportation in St. Louis. And there's not. So the three of us could ride on the bus together, and we would not be breaking any law."

They were silent.

"Just ride?" Loretta asked, finally.

"What do you mean?" I said.

"Ain't there someplace we could go?"

She surprised me. I thought riding would be enough.

"Like where?" Marlene asked.

Loretta shrugged. "Dunno," she said. "Somewhere. Ain't there any place else that ain't segregated 'cept buses?"

I had no idea.

But Marlene did. "I don't think there is, Loretta," she said. "You know, other public places, they're segregated. Parks and all. They just are. Besides, it would be fun to ride around. We could see stuff out of the bus windows, anyway."

"I would rather go someplace."

We were silent, eating. And I was thinking.

"Does Jim Crow include anybody but Negroes and white people?" I asked.

"Who else is there?" asked Marlene, wide-eyed.

"There are other people in the world, Marlene," I said.

"Yeah," said Loretta, "like the Japs, the ones we fightin'. What about them?"

"There aren't any here," Marlene said.

"Well, they got some in California," Loretta said. "Mama and me, we heard it on the news. They got some in California, and they taking away their homes and farms and stores and putting them into camps because they afraid they might be working for the enemy. And those Japs are United States citizens! Now, what do you think about that?"

"Who is 'they'?" Marlene asked.

" 'They' is the United States government, the same ones that makes up the Jim Crow laws."

"That's wrong, Loretta," I said. "The different states make up their own Jim Crow laws. The United States government doesn't have anything to do with it. It goes state by state."

"I know that," she said. "But anyway, in California, it is the main United States government taking these Jap American citizens and putting them into camps way far away from they own homes, just because we at war with Japan."

"But they are Japanese," reasoned Marlene.

"Naw," said Loretta, "they American now, but they Japanese to look at."

"So if one of them was a spy for the Japanese, you couldn't tell," countered Marlene.

"Sure you could," I said. "Citizens would have papers that said they were citizens, like my dad does. He was Canadian, and then he became an American. What if we were at war with Canada and they wanted to take all the ex-Canadians away and put them into camps—they could come and take away my father! Do you think that would be right?"

"But they couldn't," said Marlene. "He looks just like every other American."

"But that's the point!" I cried.

Loretta started to giggle.

"What is funny about this?" I demanded.

"If we was at war with Canada, they ought to come and take your father away," she laughed, "because didn't you tell us he is a spy?"

"The point is," I said, but Marlene and Loretta were howling with laughter. "The point is," I hollered, which got their attention, "that there are other people in the world besides Negroes and whites. And I'm pretty sure Jim Crow does not apply to them."

They both wiped their eyes and settled down. "So?" Marlene said.

"So we might be able to go someplace. How much money do you guys have?"

We all three were misers, it turned out. It seemed like we had saved every dime we'd ever gotten for doing chores, for birthdays, for Christmas and Chanukah, and I had hung on to the money my grandmother and aunts and uncles had slipped me when I left New York. In fact, among us, we had a lot more money than we could possibly need.

CHAPTER 12

"If Mama caught me walking through the streets with the two of you, she'd whup me to within an inch of my life," Loretta said matter-of-factly.

"So now you don't want to go?" I asked.

"I did not say that."

"She just means she has to be careful—we have to be careful—about the way we plan this," explained Marlene.

"Well, what are you thinking, then?"

"I'm thinking, first, we go to the bus by ourselves. I mean I do," Loretta answered. "I mean, we go to separate bus stops. And you two get on at one stop, and I get on at the next stop. And then we sit by ourselves for a while, just to make sure nobody who knows us gets on. And then, after we make sure, we can sit together until we get to where we are goin'. That way, my mama don't hear nothin' from nobody."

"Well, what if there is somebody we know on the bus? What do we do, just give up and go home?" I asked.

"Yes!" Marlene and Loretta said together.

"Just give up?" I cried.

"And maybe try again another day," Marlene soothed. "We don't have to take on Jim Crow and get into trouble, too, do we?"

"Walking on the street and riding on the bus together is not taking on Jim Crow," I reminded them.

"Might as well be," Loretta retorted, folding her arms stubbornly over her chest. Marlene let it be known by raising both blond brows that she agreed with Loretta.

"And what is more," Loretta continued, "I will have some tall explainin' to do anyhow, somebody see me on the bus or at the bus stop, with or without the two of you. Do not overlook that!"

It was true. Loretta was taking the biggest risk. I recognized defeat.

"Okay, okay, so let's get on with the plan. Who knows where the two closest bus stops are and what time the buses come?" I asked.

There were two stops within easy walking distance, we found out by looking at Irene's transit map and time schedule. We agreed that Loretta would walk to the closer stop, which was less than five minutes away, and that Marlene and I would go to the farther stop, about a ten-minute walk. We would get on first, and, if the coast was clear—no neighbors or anybody we knew already on the bus—we would stay seated and Loretta, waiting at the next stop, would hop on. If we met someone we knew on the bus, we would get off at the stop where Loretta was waiting. But she would get on, ride to the next stop, and then walk home. We would rendezvous back at her place.

"Seem more exciting we do run into somebody than if we don't," Loretta said. Marlene laughed. I did not.

If nobody who knew us was on the bus, Loretta would get on, and if there was nobody she knew, she would stay on, but she would not sit with us for a few stops, until we were out of our own neighborhood. Once we were far enough east—for we would be traveling east, away from Clayton and toward the city of St. Louis—Loretta, Marlene, and I planned to move to the long rear seat, where we could sit side by side, with Loretta in the middle. Or, if that back seat were taken, we would just squeeze our three selves into a regular double seat. We did not have that far to ride to get to our destination.

All this planning was necessary, just in case, but the fact was, except for the mornings when people went to work, and the evenings when they came home, the uncrowded buses did not run very often. White ladies who went downtown often took service cars—regular automobiles that ran right along the bus routes and didn't charge much more than the buses did. And most people Loretta and Irene would know, colored people, did not live anywhere around here. It would be unusual for any of us to meet someone we knew riding on the bus right smack in the middle of the day. Still, we needed to plan. You never knew—someone could get tired of waiting for a service car and just get on the bus.

We chose a Thursday when Irene would be working at her church and staying on for the potluck dinner and then for choir practice in the evening. Loretta made sure to go with her for two Thursdays in a row so when she said she didn't want to go, it would be okay with Irene if she stayed home. But since Marlene and I both were going to be away from home for a lot longer than we usually were, we had to let our mothers in on at least part of our plan.

We told them we wanted to go for a bus ride, to see something of St. Louis. We said we wanted to ride downtown and back, through some different neighborhoods, and look at the city. When we got to the end of the line, we said, we would get off the bus, cross the street, catch the same bus going in the opposite direction, and come home again.

My dad had a transit map, and I showed Mom exactly where the bus ran, where the bus stops were, what time they came and went. I pointed out to her what we would see on our way. We would go along the edge of Forest Park, catch a glimpse of Washington University, see the famous sculpture called *Meeting of the Waters* in front of the railway station. We would see the New Cathedral. We would even see the Mississippi River in between all the big downtown buildings as we waited for the bus to bring us home. At least I was pretty sure we would. And then all the things we would see that weren't on the map, all the different neighborhoods. And riding on a bus, I pointed out, we would be safe.

Mom thought it was a grand idea. "I started riding the subway in New York all by myself when I was about your age," she bragged, "or maybe I was a little older. But I know I did ride with my sister when I was your age, I remember that. And it's a lot harder to find your way around the New York City subway system than it is to take a bus downtown and back."

Marlene's mom had an agreeable sense of adventure and thought it sounded like a fun outing. "And it will be educational, too," she told the grandmothers when they objected, "like a field trip, from school." But there was one thing: we would have to take Liz with us.

"Mommy!" Marlene protested.

"But Liz will love it," her mother said, sounding puzzled. "It's just the sort of thing she enjoys, honey. Why in the world wouldn't you take her along? I'll pay her fare. Why, I'll pay yours, too, if you take her."

"It isn't that . . ."

"Then what is it?" Mrs. O'Brien asked, all innocence and concern.

"It's just . . ."

"Just?"

"I have to ask Susan."

"What did she say when you said that?" I asked.

"She smiled and said, 'I know Susan will say yes. The Marcuses are crazy about Liz.' "

"Crazy about Liz!"

"Well, she *is* Lizzy's mother," Marlene pointed out.

"Right," I said.

And that was that.

"I guess it's all off, then," I said.

"I think we should leave it up to Loretta," Marlene suggested.

"Why?"

"She might not agree."

"What do you want to bet?"

"I don't want to bet, I just want to ask her."

"Why bother? You know what she'll say as well as I do, Marlene. It's ruined. It's spoiled. Over. Forget it."

"Let's just ask Loretta, Miss Grumpus."

I was upset to begin with, and when I heard the word *grumpus*, I was ready to jump right down her throat. But then I saw that playful challenge in Marlene's pretty eyes, and I understood that no matter what, even when she was going toe-to-toe with me, she was still my friend.

"Okay." I gave in with a shrug. "Go ahead and ask her."

"You have to come with me."

"Why do I?"

"You just do, Susan. Now come on."

Grumpily, I tagged along.

"Liz?" Loretta said. "Sure. Why not?"

CHAPTER 13

We all got dressed up that day. Loretta set out for the bus stop wearing a sleeveless yellow dress with a white collar, white ankle socks and polished-up old Mary Janes, and a white straw hat with a turned-up brim. She was carrying a small white purse. I thought she looked very grown up.

Marlene and Liz were wearing identical pinafores, which their mom had made for them. Marlene's was rose-colored with white rickrack trim, and Liz's was powder blue. Marlene had a black purse one of the grandmothers had crocheted, with a long skinny strap so she could carry it slung across her chest, like ammunition.

I had on a cap-sleeved, white blouse and a navy blue skirt with navy blue–and–white polka-dotted belt. The skirt buttoned all the way down the front and had deep pockets on either side, and each pocket buttoned closed with a great big white button. Into one pocket, I had slipped the brown leather coin purse with the fake gold snap Mom loaned me to put my bus fare in. She didn't know about the rest of the money I was bringing, which I had folded up, secured with a rubber band, and dropped into the other pocket.

Cranky Liz would not keep up, and before we could get ourselves across Clayton Road, we saw our bus lumbering toward the stop. Nobody was waiting where we had planned to be waiting, so the driver just kept on going. *Now what? Now what?* a voice screamed inside my head.

I turned to Marlene, panicked. *Just stay calm,* she signaled with her eyebrows. And the three of us held hands and carefully crossed the wide road.

We had to wait a long time for the next bus, and the whole time I fretted about what might or might not have happened at the next stop down the line. Had Loretta seen in time that we were not on board, or had she gotten on and paid her fare and then noticed? And then what? Had she gotten off at the next stop and gone home? Or had she just gone home in the first place, never boarding the bus at all?

Because of Liz, our day was ruined—*as I had predicted.*

"Maybe she waited, just in case," Marlene whispered to me.

"Why would she do that?" I whispered back. "That would not be what we planned."

"I know," Marlene said, "but we made the plan before Liz was coming. Loretta might just guess that something like this would happen, once Liz was involved."

The three of us climbed aboard the next bus, when it finally came, and after Marlene and I looked all up and down—it was practically empty, and we did not know any of the few people on it—we sat down close to the front, so we could see if Loretta was still waiting at the next stop.

Liz, completely unconcerned, made her way to the back of the bus and plopped herself down.

As the bus approached the next stop, we practically hugged each other. There was Loretta, standing very straight with her purse over her arm and her white hat on, looking like a grown-up, but small. She put her hands up over her eyes, shielding them from the sun, and watched it come.

"She waited!" Marlene whispered. "She waited! What did I tell you?"

"She broke the rules," I grumbled, smiling.

"She did," Marlene agreed happily.

"Why did we even bother to make any?" I asked, a bit put out.

Marlene smiled at me, her clear eyes showing no confusion at all. "I don't know, Susan," she said. "Maybe that is what they mean when they say, 'rules are made to be broken.'"

I had never heard anyone say that. "Marlene, did you just make that up?" I demanded.

"No, honest, it's a saying. I've heard people say it. I think it means you have to think for yourself, like Loretta did."

The bus wheezed to a halt and the doors folded open. Loretta stepped up the big steps, almost too high for her, and put her nickel into the fare box. Then she walked past us and sat down by herself in the middle section of the bus. She was back to following the plan again.

But Liz was not.

"Hey, Loretta," she called, "come sit back here with me!"

CHAPTER 14

We all sat together on the long backseat of the bus, whispering and giggling. We didn't have far to ride to get to our stop, the one near the Esquire Movie Theater.

Every time the bus bounced, the backseat bounced extra hard, it seemed, and Liz made much out of how bumpy and bouncy it was in the back of the bus, bumping and bouncing her silly self all over the place, and giggling so hard that she made the rest of us laugh, too.

The few people who were riding in the seats in front of us turned around to see who was making all the noise. *Just kids*, I felt like telling them, *having a good time*. But from their sour-looking faces, you could see they were thinking about something else.

Too bad. We knew we weren't breaking any rules. It was not against the law for the four of us to be riding on the bus together. And it was not against the law for us to be having fun.

"Our stop," Marlene said. You could see the movie marquee from the bus window. We jumped up and stood in line by the back door, which, after the bus wheezed to a stop, swooshed open.

"Come on, Liz," I said. But Liz lagged, and she looked confused.

"Why are we getting off?" she asked, holding back. It dawned on me only then that Marlene had not told her the whole plan. "Why are we getting off so soon?" Liz whined.

"Just come on, Liz," I said, "right now. Hurry." Marlene and Loretta were already on the sidewalk, and I was halfway down the stairs. "Liz, come on! The door's going to close!"

"Liz," they called, "get off the bus!"

The urgency in our voices propelled her down the stairs behind me and onto the sidewalk, and as soon as we both were off the bus, the driver closed the door and roared away.

"What was wrong? Why did we get off? We are nowhere near downtown, are we? We have not seen anything you told Mom we were going to see!" Liz confronted her sister.

I put myself between them. "Calm down, Liz," I said.

"I will not calm down." She stamped her foot.

"Lizzy," Marlene began. But that was as far as she got.

"Lizzy what?" demanded Liz.

"You girls do take the cake," Loretta remarked. "You have not told Liz about the plan, now, have you?"

"Well, it wasn't my job," I replied. "She's not my responsibility."

We both looked at Marlene, who made a helpless face. "I was afraid to," she confessed. "She would have told Mom."

"I never!" objected Liz. "I never!" Then, "Told Mom what?"

"That we were not just going for a bus ride—that we have another plan."

"We do?"

We all nodded.

"What is it?"

We were standing on the sidewalk, shouting. Anybody passing by—if anybody had been passing by—could have easily overheard everything we said.

"Shhh," I said, and motioned that we should stand closer to one another. We huddled together.

"What is it?" said Liz in a croaky whisper.

"We are going to strike a blow against Jim Crow," I said.

Liz looked blank.

"We are going to—um—break a rule, maybe," said Marlene.

Liz looked interested.

"We eating lunch at a Chinese restaurant," said Loretta.

Liz looked flummoxed. "A what?" she asked.

"A Chinese restaurant," Marlene said.

"We're eating lunch at a restaurant?" Liz asked, after a pause. We all nodded, yes.

"By ourselves?"

Yes.

"For money?"

"I have money," Marlene assured her. "For both of us."

"Chinese?"

Yes.

"Chinese food?"

Yes.

"But what kind of food is that? Why are we doing this? I don't want to eat Chinese food. I want to—"

"Liz?" said Loretta.

"Yes?"

"Be quiet."

"But—"

"No buts, Liz. We ain't got all day. We executin' a plan. And you lucky to be in on it. So button up your lip."

"What's the plan?" asked Liz.

"We *integratin'* a restaurant," Loretta told her. "And you ever dare tell about it, you gonna get what-for. Understand?"

Liz did not say another word.

"Now," Loretta said, turning to me, "which way do we go to get to where we goin'?"

I hesitated. "I'm pretty sure it's over that way."

"Pretty sure?"

"Well, I can't tell from here, Loretta. I have to get to the movie theater first and then see. Mom and Daddy and I always go there after we get out of the movie. I have to start from there."

"Let's march," she said.

And march we did, two by two, Loretta and Liz behind me and Marlene, and nobody dawdling, until we stood in front of the Esquire, where we all stopped.

"Okay," Loretta said, hands on her hips, the white purse hanging off one skinny wrist, "now where?"

I looked around. "Hmmm," I said, frowning thoughtfully, and trying to look as if I knew what I was looking at. But somehow the streets all looked the same and I realized that I had never paid much attention to where I was going when I walked to the Chinese restaurant with my parents. I had just gone along with them, thinking my own thoughts, and I had ended up believing I knew where we'd gone—which direction, how far—but in fact, I had no idea.

"Now where, Susan?" Marlene prompted. I took a deep breath.

"Over this way," I said, choosing a direction and hoping it was the right one. "It's about five or six blocks down this way." Off we marched again.

As we walked, I looked for anything familiar that would tell me I had chosen the right way, but nothing—absolutely nothing—caught my eye. And with each passing block, my heart sank lower, and I scanned both sides of the street more and more frantically for Chinese writing on a storefront restaurant window.

"That's five blocks," Loretta announced, as we passed the fifth corner and crossed the street.

"Yep," I said, trying to sound calm, "it should be in this next block or the next one." Soon I would have to admit I'd taken us the wrong way. The only thing that was giving me any hope at all was the way the neighborhood was deteriorating. That much I did remember. As Mom and Daddy and I walked to the restaurant, the streets had gotten dirtier and dirtier and the houses and stores had looked more and more run-down. But I knew that might have happened in any direction I'd chosen to walk from the Esquire.

"That's six blocks," announced merciless Loretta. We all stopped.

"There it is, I think," said Marlene. "Isn't that Chinese writing over there?" She pointed across the street and a few storefronts down.

"Yes!" I cried with relief. We crossed the deserted street.

CHAPTER
15

As we hurried toward the Chinese restaurant, I was disappointed to see that it didn't appear to be open. It had never occurred to me that it might not be. And when we got right up to it, I found out why: Half of the plate glass window had been smashed and was covered over with cardboard and newspaper. The other half had a big crack running across the glass from one end to the other, and on it, in thick black paint, someone had written, JAPS GO HOME!

JAP TRAITOR was written in black paint on the sidewalk in front of the restaurant. And paint had been thrown all around, on the sidewalk and on the building. Tiny bits of shattered glass, too small to clean up, sparkled in the street and on the sidewalk.

Standing there, I had the creepiest feeling that whoever did this was still around, maybe watching us. Marlene must have felt the same way. "Let's get out of here," she said.

But Loretta and Liz did not budge.

"Come on," Marlene quietly urged, and she and I took a few steps back.

Liz, however, moved closer to the window and peered through it into the darkened space.

"What are you doing, Liz?" I hissed.

Loretta stood like a statue between us and Liz. She seemed not to know which way to go, or which of us to side with.

"Liz," Marlene whispered as loudly as you can whisper, "come over here. We're leaving."

But Liz didn't pay any attention to anyone. We couldn't even tell if she heard us. She glued her eyes to the cracked glass and stared inside.

Suddenly, the restaurant door burst open. We all jumped. Loretta scurried over to stand next to Marlene and me.

A small Chinese man in a food-spattered white cook's jacket burst out screaming, "Go! Go away! I call police!"

I recognized him. He was the owner of the restaurant who had talked, or tried to talk, to my father every time we ate there.

I stepped toward him. "It's just me," I said loudly. "Remember me?"

But he yelled, "Go, go! I call police!"

"No! Wait!" I yelled back. "It's just me—remember—*me*! I ate here with my parents!"

Then behind him, another voice, a woman's voice. Now even Liz backed away. The woman, the owner's wife who had shown me the blue willow plates and tried to tell me the story, came screeching out. She had a cleaver in her hand and she was waving it and crying, "Call police! Kill you! Go way!"

And he was yelling, "Not Jap! Chinee! Not Jap!"

And Liz was frozen, and Marlene and Loretta were screaming, too. "Susan, come on! Susan, let's go! Susan, Susan!" But I walked right up to them, and yelled right back at them. "Wait! Stop! I know you! Don't you know who I am?"

And suddenly the woman looked out over her husband's shoulder and saw me—and I could see her see me—and she stopped yelling and lowered the cleaver and said something to him in Chinese. And he stopped yelling and peered and squinted at me. And then they both started to smile, and then to laugh. And then they bowed little Chinese bows of welcome, hello, hello, and they opened the door, bowing and saying things in Chinese, and then they looked out and saw the others—Liz standing frozen a few feet away and Loretta and Marlene, wide-eyed and frightened a little farther down the sidewalk, and then said, "Come, come, okay now, okay now." And the others looked at me, and even though I wasn't completely sure, I took a very deep breath and called, "It's all right. Come on."

And very slowly, very cautiously, my friends walked toward the restaurant. I went in first, by myself. The woman turned on the lights, and she pointed around at the empty tables, as if to say choose one. I waited for the others. "Where do you want to sit?" I asked them, as they huddled together in the doorway.

We chose a table in the center of the tiny room.

The man said, "I make lunch," and he disappeared into the kitchen. And the woman brought us a teapot full of steaming hot black tea and some chopsticks, and forks, too.

After a while, platters full of hot food appeared at our table. Soup. Noodles. Chicken. Fish. Vegetables. Each one had a Chinese name, but we could not remember it for more than a second. We ate off the blue willow plates, and there was far more food than we could hope to finish. And at the end, orange sherbet and fortune cookies: special folded-over vanilla cookies with skinny pieces of paper baked inside them. And on the pieces of paper, a fortune was printed.

The four cookies were delivered to the table on one plate, and you had to choose which one was yours. Liz grabbed one.

But Loretta and Marlene and I hesitated. "Go ahead," I said, very politely.

"No, you go," Loretta said, just as politely.

Marlene took hers.

Loretta closed her eyes and took hers.

And I took mine.

Sometimes the fortunes I got when I went with my parents had a lot to do with me. And sometimes they had nothing to do with me.

Liz broke her cookie open, stuffed half of it into her mouth, and tried to read her fortune: "What're these words?" she asked Marlene. Marlene looked at her piece of paper. " 'Only patience,' " she said. Liz started again. " 'Only patience can bring . . .' " Marlene helped her again: " 'Happiness.' "

" 'Only patience can bring happiness?' " Liz cried. "What kind of a fortune is that? I am never patient! And I am always happy. I think I got somebody else's fortune. Who wants to trade?"

"You can't trade, Liz," I said, giggling.

"No fair," she said, crumpling up her fortune and gobbling down the rest of the cookie. She folded her arms on the table and put her chin down on them.

Loretta opened hers. " 'Friendship must be cared for and watered like a plant,' " she read. We thought about that, and we nodded in agreement.

"Cared for," Marlene said, "like the plants in a garden, so it will grow."

Even Liz seemed to like it. Loretta folded the piece of paper and put it into her purse. She nibbled the fortune cookie, made a face, and did not eat it.

"Can I have it?" asked Liz. Loretta pushed it over to her, and Liz gobbled it down.

"You next, Susan," said Marlene. I slowly broke open my cookie and unfolded the pink slip of paper. " 'The future sleeps in the present.' "

"What does that mean? Can I have your cookie?" said Liz.

"No," I said, "I'm eating it."

"It means sort of like a seed in the garden," Loretta ventured. "The seed is the present, and the plant that grows out of it is the future."

"Or what you do now affects what happens to you later," Marlene suggested.

Both of those made sense to me. I put the fortune in my pocket and ate the cookie.

Marlene carefully cracked her cookie open. Her fortune was on blue paper. " 'Friendship lives beyond time and place,' " she read.

"That means we will be friends forever," Liz said, "even after we die. Can I have your cookie?"

"No."

"Well, anyway, do you think that's what it means?"

"I don't know about the 'after we die' part," I said, "but friends forever, I think that's what it means."

"Okay, me too, then," Liz said. "Forget about 'after we die.' "

"You got the best fortune, Marlene," Liz said. "You always get the best things." She didn't sound jealous. She was just stating a fact.

Marlene smiled in agreement.

I was so full, I wasn't sure I would be able to get up. And Marlene whispered to me, "Do you think we have enough money to pay for all this food?"

"I think so," I said. "Daddy always talks about how inexpensive it is to eat here."

While we were eating, a couple of other people came to the door. Each time, the wife went and greeted them, less afraid now, it seemed, since someone was already inside the restaurant having a meal.

"Chinee," she said smiling to each of the people. "Chinee. Come in?" And two of them did. Having us there, right in the middle of the restaurant having such a good time, with the smells of the food going out the door and onto the street, seemed to attract some business, in spite of the broken glass and the nasty writing all over the front.

Finally, we got our check. Everything we had eaten was represented in Chinese writing, which we all took turns looking at, it was so strange and interesting. And the total amount we owed was written down at the bottom. $00.00. Nothing!

"They are not charging us for our lunch!" Marlene said.

"That's not right!" Loretta said.

"What's not right about it?" Liz wanted to know.

I had to think. First of all, we had no way of knowing what to pay, if they did not charge us. We had never seen a menu; they had just served us what they wanted to. And second, I understood why they didn't want to charge us. We had done them a favor by coming into the restaurant, and by making it possible for other people to come back and eat here. They were thanking us.

"We can't pay for lunch if they don't want to charge us," I said. "But we can leave them a big tip."

We agreed to that. And each of us left them a whole dollar, which is what we had planned to spend for lunch in the first place.

The Chinese lady went the few steps to the front door with us, and the man came out of the kitchen to stand next to her in the doorway. He waved. "Chinee," he said, smiling.

We smiled. "Thanks for lunch," Liz said, sticking her stomach out so she looked like a fat lady and rubbing it. This made them laugh.

The four of us hurried away. Our adventure was over, and suddenly we all felt tired and ready to go home.

"Look," Marlene said, as we hurried toward the Esquire and the bus stop. Across the street from the restaurant was a Chinese laundry, also with broken windows, also with JAP GO HOME written across the window. We walked even more quickly. Being back out on the street made us feel the same sense of danger we'd felt before.

"And so what if they was Japanese?" Loretta asked. "Ain't this what we was talkin' about the other day?"

"What?" asked Liz.

"Not you," Marlene said, "you weren't talking about it. We were."

"Well, if they were Japanese, we would've had Japanese food for lunch," said Liz, "that's what."

Everybody laughed, and here came our bus, more crowded this time, because it had gotten a lot later than we'd thought it would. We looked at one another. Should we all get on, or should we play it safe?

But when the bus stopped and the doors opened, Liz scrambled aboard, and then as the three of us stood hesitating on the sidewalk, she turned to Loretta and said, "Well, come on, pokey." And Loretta went up the steps, so there was no reason for Marlene and me not to follow.

It was the wrong thing to do.

Because—of all people!—there was Aunt Helen sitting right smack in the front seat. Liz was still acting silly, doing her fat lady walk and giggling, and she went right by Aunt Helen. Loretta kept her eyes straight ahead, and even though I could see from the way her shoulders and her neck tightened up that she saw Aunt Helen, she just kept going and pretended not to.

Marlene smiled as she went by. "Hello, Mrs. Goodman," she said. And then, just as I was ready to do the same, the bus started up with a tremendous jerk, and since I wasn't holding on to anything, I grabbed the closest thing, which happened to be Marlene, and then she and I both toppled halfway over, right onto Aunt Helen, and then, as the bus picked up speed, it set us back on our feet again, in the aisle, where we belonged.

We had knocked Aunt Helen's hat sideways on her head, and she stared furiously up at us, the fashionable hat askew with its bunch of fake bright red cherries now hanging down in her face.

"Hello, Aunt Helen," I said, blushing bright and hot. "Sorry!"

Marlene and I walked as quickly as we could to the back of the bus, and when Liz started her bouncing and giggling, Marlene whispered, "Stop it, Liz, or else!"

Even Liz could tell she meant business, and, pouting, she folded her arms over her chest and sat still.

Every once in a while, Aunt Helen, her hat adjusted, would turn her whole self around and peer at us, as if she was making sure she had seen what she thought she had, as if she could not really trust her own eyes. She would stare good and hard at the four of us, frown and shake her head, and then turn around and face front again.

And every time she did that, Loretta, who was sitting perfectly straight with her head unnaturally still and high, would frown and let her scared eyes slide over to look at Marlene and me, and Liz would roll her eyes up toward the top of the bus and start to hum, and then Marlene would fake-smile and push her elbow into Liz's side and say through almost closed lips, "Liz, I am *warning* you!" And I would just sit, too unhappy to say or do anything.

The ride was too short. Before I knew it, the territory outside began to look familiar. I closed my eyes. But then, Marlene cried, "Susan! Look!"

"At what?" I said, not opening even one eye the tiniest little bit.

"Susan!" she cried again.

"Looky, Susan!" said Liz.

"Lord lord lord!" That was Loretta.

I opened my eyes. And then shot up straight in my seat. It was our stop up ahead. And there, parked right smack in the bus stop where no car was supposed to be, was Uncle Lou's dark blue Buick. And there, standing right next to the car was Uncle Lou—that tall, whale-shaped man, wearing a short-sleeved white shirt with his tie pulled down and his straw summer hat pushed onto the back of his head, shading his eyes with one hand and waving like mad with the other, as if the bus might not stop if he didn't flag it down, even though he and his car were right there in its path.

Everybody on the bus could hear the driver muttering.

And everybody could hear Aunt Helen exclaim, "Why, there is my husband! Be careful! Don't run him down!"

This set all the passengers laughing, and then the driver said loudly and very sarcastically, "No, ma'am, I won't run him down, even if the darn fool has parked himself and his automobile right where this bus is supposed to be going."

And that made the passengers laugh even more.

But the driver did a good job of bringing the bus to a stop right next to where Uncle Lou was standing and waving his arms around, and then he opened the door of the bus and leaned over and Uncle Lou called, "Driver, I am looking for my wife, she—Oh, there you are, Helen!" he exclaimed, and he hopped on to the bus and took her and her packages into his arms and half dragged and half carried the astonished woman off the bus and somehow got her into the front seat of the parked Buick. As he went around to the driver's side of the car, he waved to the bus driver—and blew him a kiss! Then he revved his engine as if he were a teenager, and peeled away.

The dumbfounded passengers all were silent. Including us. We were so stunned, instead of getting off the bus, we just sat there.

"Now don't that beat all?" inquired the driver. He took off his peaked cap and, with a huge white handkerchief, he wiped the perspiration off the leather band inside it and set it back on his head. Then he looked around. "Anybody else need to get off here?" he asked.

"We do!" we cried, walking up and practically falling over each other in our haste to get to the rear door.

He opened it, and we stumbled down the high steps. We were scarcely on the sidewalk when he roared away.

There we stood, surrounded by bus fumes, hot and tired,

not quite ready to trudge home and face the music when up screeched the Buick. Aunt Helen, her face wet with tears, beamed at us from the rolled-down passenger window, and Uncle Lou leaped out of the driver's seat and rushed over to us on the sidewalk.

"I had no idea you kids were on that bus!" he exclaimed. "Would never have just left you like that!" He opened the back door of the car. "Hop in, hop in!" He pushed the air all around the four of us with his hands. Liz jumped right in.

"Gee, thanks!" she said.

I could see Loretta holding back. "Come on, girls, come on!" he urged. "Let's go, gotta go, gotta go!"

And Aunt Helen was looking out and smiling, too, and she said, "It's all right, girls, get into the car. Everything is all right now. Everything finally is all right. We have the most wonderful news!"

"Wonderful news!" Uncle Lou echoed as he ran back around and jumped into the driver's seat. "He's been found!" he said as the car lurched forward. "Found!"

Their son, Allen, Missing In Action, had turned up that very day. Uncle Lou had gotten a telephone call from him at work late that morning, while Aunt Helen was downtown shopping, and he had been waiting at the bus stop—waiting on bus after bus after bus until finally the one she was riding had come along—so he could tell her the extraordinary, unexpected good news: Their son was no longer Missing.

What had happened was this: Many months before, Allen's unit in Europe was in danger of being captured. His commanding officer was so sure they'd be captured, he told the Jewish soldiers to ditch their dog tags. A letter showing your religion was stamped on your dog tag. P for Protestant, C for

Catholic, and H for Hebrew, or Jewish. The officer was afraid the Germans would kill the Jewish soldiers instead of taking them prisoner.

So Allen followed orders and threw away his only identification. In the battle that followed, Allen's group got scattered, and Allen was wounded. Then he was sent from one hospital to another, and nobody had any way of knowing who he was. And he was too hurt to tell them.

After months and months, when Allen finally was better and able to communicate, he identified himself. And then, after even more delays—there was still a war going on, after all—he was able to call home. So that was what happened. Allen had been badly hurt but he was in a hospital, recovering. He wasn't coming home right away. But he wasn't Missing anymore, either.

That night, a lot of people came over to Aunt Helen and Uncle Lou's, just drifted over and stayed awhile. Gave Aunt Helen a hug. Shook Uncle Lou's hand. Relatives came, and friends. Neighbors. Mrs. O'Brien brought over a plate of cookies. And when Irene got home and Loretta told her what had happened, Irene went out into her twilight purply garden and picked the last of the summer berries and brought them up the back stairs. Uncle Lou was in the kitchen when she came, and he invited her in to clink glasses of iced tea with him, to celebrate.

After that, Irene let Loretta come up to my house, and she and I sat in my front doorway and looked into Aunt Helen and Uncle Lou's through the adjacent front doors, both open, and watched all the happy people coming and going, and listened to the murmur of laughing and crying and talking.

We both got tired early, though. Unknown to anyone else, we'd had a busy day.

Loretta just about sleepwalked home down the back stairs, and I went inside and slid my tired self under the Missouri Star–pattern summer quilt that now covered my bed.

And as I settled down, I realized with woozy relief: Nobody was ever going to ask us a single thing about where we'd been that day, or what we'd done. Yet we had eaten in a public place, white and colored together!

We had defied Jim Crow, and we were going to get away with it.

Take that, Jim Crow, I thought as I fell asleep.

CHAPTER 16

When Loretta was leaving, I offered her my Victory ball. She took it and rolled it between her hands, but then she handed it back to me.

"That old backwoods farm ain't no place for a ball like this," she said. "But thanks."

"Loretta, you're not going to be there forever."

Loretta shrugged.

"You're not," I insisted. "Before you know it, you're going to be out in Oakland, California, with your mom. And I bet there's plenty of concrete out there. It will be a perfect place for a tennis ball. Here, take it." I handed it back to her. "Anyway, I want you to have it, to remember me by."

"I ain't never going to forget you, Susan," Loretta said, "not never. You know that."

"Me too." I blushed. "But still, I want you to have it, okay?"

She took the ball. "Okay," she said.

"Let's go, Loretta," Irene was calling. Somebody had come to pick them up and take them to the Greyhound bus station. They had their clothes packed in two cardboard suitcases, and Irene was carrying the bedquilt in her arms, like a baby. They had food for the trip in a shoe box with a lid on it. They both had on their best, including the hats they wore to church.

Some old man named Clarence was taking over Irene's job, and he moved into their apartment as soon as they left. Now their furniture was his furniture, and their garden was his garden. Whatever they left behind was his.

I could not stay asleep that night. It was hot and muggy, and even though I changed my sweaty pajamas and my sheet, I could not cool off. Usually when I am up at night, I just lie in my bed and think until I fall asleep again, and sometimes I'm not sure I have fallen asleep again, except I hear the morning birdsong and see the early light and remember my dreams, and then I know I did sleep.

But this time, I knew I was up. And I had the feeling somebody else was, too.

I got out of bed and stepped into the short hallway that connected my bedroom to the living room and there was Daddy, sitting on the couch in his pajamas, holding a glass of iced tea in one hand, frowning into the darkness. I stood still and watched him.

"Come in, Susie-Q," he finally said, and I came in and sat next to him. He set the iced tea down on the end table and put his arm around the back of the couch behind me.

"What's keeping you awake?" he asked.

I shrugged. "You?" I asked.

"Thoughts," he said.

"What about?"

"Things."

"Now Loretta is gone, too," I complained.

"Mmmm."

"And I will never see her again, either, I bet."

"Probably not."

"Just like Marv." My voice did something funny, and Daddy gave me a pat.

"Well, that is kind of what I was thinking about, too," he said.

"Marv?"

"Not Marv. But I was thinking about what is going on in the world right now. About how many people are separated from people they care about and don't know whether they will ever see them again or not."

"You were thinking about the war, Daddy," I explained.

He nodded.

"But I was just thinking about me and my friends."

"That's about the war, too, Susan. We would never be here if not for the war. I would still have my job in New York, and you and your mother would still have your lives there." He paused. Then he quickly added, "Of course, that is nothing compared to the complications and the sadness the war has caused in other people's lives. You and I know that, don't we?"

I thought about the Chinese restaurant people and about Allen. About the newsreels we saw at the movies that showed bombings and crashes and fires and rubble and battles and people just walking with no place to go and frightened children and dead bodies. I knew that moving to Clayton and even that never seeing Marv again was a tiny complication compared to what was happening to other people. I knew it. But I am selfish, and sometimes I don't feel it. I still sometimes felt sad about what happened to me.

Daddy studied my gloomy face. "I believe those bangs have grown out," he remarked companionably.

I had to smile into the dark. They had. And just in the nick of time. School would be starting any minute.

CHAPTER 17

Marlene and Liz came to pick me up on the first day of school. I should have picked them up, since their house was on my way, but they were ready sooner and showed up at our door. The problem was, Mom was trying to make me wear a wintery dress, with puffy sleeves and a stiff white collar, that I knew would be way too hot. So I was standing in my underwear and my socks and my new black-and-white saddle shoes, arguing with my mother, when they knocked.

Mom got the door. "Susan's not ready," she told them, in a kind of helpless voice that seemed to say, *and I can't imagine why.*

"She has to be ready or we are all going to be late," Liz said, stepping right past my mother into our apartment. "Susan!" Liz cried. "You're not even dressed yet? Hurry up!"

Liz was wearing her dirty, worn-out summer sneakers and no socks and a plain, cool blouse and the dirndl skirt she and her mother had made over the summer, her first sewing project. It had not turned out very well, but Liz loved it. Her hair was a rat's nest. She seemed to have forgotten to brush it in her excitement about getting to school and somehow to have eluded the grandmothers, too. "Susan, get dressed," she commanded.

I glared at my mother, who stood holding the red plaid dress.

Marlene was wearing a sleeveless blouse and a pale pink wraparound summer skirt with bobby sox and the same black-and-white saddle shoes as mine—we had gone shopping with our mothers and picked them out together. She had stepped into the front hall, but she did not barge into our apartment the way Liz did.

Now Liz actually rummaged around in my closet. "Here," she said, whipping a sleeveless summer dress off its hanger. "Put this on and let's get going." I took it from her and threw it over my head before Mom could say a word.

"Got your lunch?" Liz asked.

"Mom wants me to come home for lunch," I said from under the dress. When I emerged, I saw Marlene roll her eyes behind my mother's back.

"Nobody goes home for lunch!" exclaimed Liz. She turned to my mother. "Nobody!" she repeated. "But if Susan doesn't have a lunch to take, she can buy lunch today in the cafeteria. Just give her twenty-five cents. They have all kinds of good stuff for lunch. And if the cafeteria isn't open yet, I will share my lunch with her." She waved her brown bag in my startled mother's direction, and Mom went to get twenty-five cents, which she handed to me without a word.

"And don't forget," Liz said, "milk money tomorrow. Ten cents for milk money, they collect on Tuesdays. Or is it Mondays?" She thought. "Well, this week it will be Tuesday, because there will be too many kids who don't remember about it today. So, are you ready now?" she said to me impatiently.

Marlene rolled her eyes again and almost laughed, and this time so did Mom. I stood at attention and saluted. "Ready,

Liz," I said. And, in a much better mood, I gave my mother a kiss, and she gave me and Liz and Marlene each a little off-you-go hug, and off we went, tearing down the stairs so fast that she called, "Be careful, girls!" and we laughed loudly about nothing, and our laughter bounced around the stairwell and followed us out into the warm, dusty, end-of-summer, first-day-of-school September morning.

Kids were all over the place and all heading in the same direction.

And when we got to the top of our sloping street, I could see more streets feeding into other streets on either side of us and streets coming toward us, and on all the streets, I could see kids—kids walking by themselves, and kids walking in twos and threes, big kids shepherding little ones, and some little ones resolutely marching along on their own. And in the clear, warm, soft morning air there was a sense of excitement and urgency. Nobody was late, nobody was running. And yet all those kids, all us kids, were walking with eager intention toward the school, as if we were being pulled there by a magnet.

And from every direction, children came, more and more and more of them, drawn by the magnet of the school—with its spacious hallways and tall windows and new books and art supplies, its big playground and its sloping green lawn. It drew us to it from all over the neighborhood, and as I walked toward it and saw other children walking too, I had the feeling that I could also see us from someplace high up, like from the top of the Wonder Wheel at Coney Island, a big amusement park in New York—and from way up high on top of the Wonder Wheel I could see the school and I could see children coming toward it. Children I didn't know. Children I was going to get to know. New friends.

And I remembered Marlene's fortune cookie: "Friendship lives beyond time and place." That would be my friendship with Marv and Rose and now Loretta, too. And I remembered Loretta's fortune cookie: "Friendship must be cared for and watered like a plant." That would be my friendship with Marlene and Liz, and with the new friends I was going to make.

I tried to remember the other two fortunes, but I couldn't—there was just too much going on. Because now all of us were converging on the Glenview School at once, filling the wide, light hallways with our exuberant selves.

Liz took off with some other second-graders who were just as rambunctious as she was. And Marlene smiled her glorious smile and took my hand, and together we ran up the stairs to our fifth-grade classroom.